Auth

Usually when you find a ch one of Robby's stories, it's h in an autobiorgraphical way. However, in this narrative, the only thing Robby and Boz share in common is that Robby wrote the song atrributed to Boz, For You the World Was Made.

However, the appearance of Boz in Robby's other books will indicate that Robby was born, and spend much of his life in Thailand and lives in Northern Ireland. In Thailand, he did such things as teach English, help with various projects including a shelter for homeless children, did telemarketting, and did missionary work (like his parents).

Right now, he lives in Northern Ireland with his wife Bless (also from Thailand), and his son Abe, who also has ideas for a few novels. Apart from his day job, he also designs his own and other people's books in ebook and print format.

He also designed the cover. Isn't it lovely?

He doesn't have a cat.

Visit him at *www.RobbyCharters.co.uk* and download a free copy of ***The Wrong Time***

Rat in the Cellar

by Robby Charters

© 2021 by Robby Charters

Front Cover and interior design and formatting by:
www.Robbys-eBook-Formatting.co.uk

Disclamers

This is a work of fiction. Any resemblance of fictional characters to actual persons living, dead, or yet to be born, is entirely fictional.

Chapter 1

Oscar's house was the oldest in the neighbourhood. It was the only one that wasn't destroyed by the riots five years ago, when the whole neighbourhood had to be rebuilt. Some of the neighbours stayed, but a lot of new people moved in. Oscar could barely remember that.

Before that, it was the only one spared the great fire that happened way before Oscar was born. Before that again, it survived the big earthquake, which was quite amazing because, looking at it, you wouldn't have thought it was built with earthquakes in mind. A couple of the other houses that were certified earthquake proof, toppled. Engineers were amazed.

In one of the bombing raids during the war, the one old Gandpa Nick fought in before Oscar's granddad was born, this neighbourhood was leveled - all but this house. Again, the neighbourhood was rebuilt.

Nobody was sure when the house was built. Some said it was Victorian, but the style wasn't quite right for that. Daddy thought it was an old farmhouse, but Uncle Charlie didn't think so. He was the architect of the family. But it had all sorts of features, some that no one had ever seen before.

One was a staircase that seemed to go up to the attic, but there was no attic in that part of the house. Another was a stairwell down in the cellar that also seemed to be a dead end. When they shone a light down, it didn't look like it went anywhere. No one thought it was safe to venture down. No one enjoyed being in those parts of the house anyway. Even the previous owner had recommended boarding up both stairways, but they never got around to it. The cellar went unused, as the age of giant coal furnaces was long past and the kitchen had plenty of space for both washer and dryer. The two main floors were room enough for a family of four (five when Uncle Milton lived there). Oscar was told never to play on either set of the dead-end stairs.

No one envied the Daugherty family for living there. Some of the older residents of the neighbourhood, ones who had survived a few renovations, thought it used to have the reputation of being haunted. It had sat empty for long periods of time. One family that lived there about 100 years ago was thought to have disappeared. No estate agents ever made offers like they often did for other old houses. The council never even thought of having it listed in spite of the age and strange design.

But Oscar's family did just fine there, as long as they stuck to the two main floors. No one ever ventured to the cellar or the third level except the cat.

The cat had just appeared in the house about the time Oscar was six, and lived with them a while, sometimes disappearing for long periods, and then coming back. Oscar was fond of that cat. It was fond of Oscar, and used to jump onto his bed at night and purr loudly in his ear, which he found especially soothing. But when Oscar was eight, it disappeared again and, so far, hadn't returned. That was a year ago.

Right now, it was just the three of them, Mum, Dad and Oscar. Megan was away at University, where she was most of the time since before Uncle Milton was carted off to prison.

Oscar wasn't sure what Uncle Milton was in for. Before that, there seemed to be some issue between him and

Megan; and her going off to University seemed to solve the problem.

Megan came home on holidays, and other times when the Universities and schools had to be closed because of political problems, and riots, and pandemics - maybe war...

Daddy said that if not for the prospect of war with 'our noble neighbours', the nation would be in a civil war.

Some politician, who actually wasn't a politician but a businessman, used to support one of the new radical parties, and even became a cabinet minister. Later, he formed his own party, promised a lot of things to the more conservative and low income people, and won the following election by a landslide.

The way he did things won the hearts of the poor and the conservatives, but it upset a lot of people in the establishment, as well as the more educated types.

Because he did some things that were considered illegal and against protocol, some of the key powers that together, had veto power, kicked him out. The 'billionaire politician' had to flee the country. A coalition government took over, but in the next election, the same party won again. The new leader was a follower of the earlier one who was in exile. Again they were thrown out. Then came the 'Red Bandana' riots. Supporters of the billionaire politician distinguished themselves by wearing red bandanas.

That had been the story of the country since before Oscar was born.

But now most of the attention was on 'our noble neighbours'. In the era of wind generators and solar panels, they were still fighting over oilfields and mineral resources. The border areas were rich in those, so the rich businessmen on both sides - the ones who pulled the strings and paid their politicians - had conflicting opinions about what land belonged to who.

Other countries were also fighting it out. One had gone nuclear - using a 'clean' neutron bomb.

That didn't leave a radioactive mess in its wake. That's why it was called 'clean'. It also didn't destroy a whole city like the ones that took out Nagasaki and Heroshima. It only covered something like a suburb, or a section of town. The buildings and hard objects stayed, for the most part, intact. Only biological organisms disintegrated - people, cats, dogs.

Before the age of the 'billionaire politician', the previous leader was very influential in inviting people to peace talks, and stopping potential wars. Since that time, things seemed to have got out of hand.

Oscar's room was at the end of the corridor next to the stairs to the top floor.

He had only ever been to the top floor once, when he looked up the forbidden stairs. That was in the middle of the night, when he was sure he heard footsteps going up the stairs.

He got out of bed and went up. He found a corridor just like the one on the floor his bedroom was on, except no carpet. All the doors were locked except the bathroom. The corridor turned to the left. More locked rooms. One of the locked doors led to the real attic. Up ahead was the opening to the stairs to nowhere.

No one was on those stairs. He hadn't heard any doors being locked or unlocked.

He was spooked.

He asked his parents if he could sleep between them in their bed, but they told him he was getting too old for that.

Later, the cat jumped on to his bed and purred him to sleep. That was the last time he saw the cat. Again, that was a year ago.

School had been closed for a few days, but not dad and mum's jobs.

They were lucky to have jobs. So many people had lost theirs, but even then, they were paid so little they both had to do overtime to pay the bills. Dad had two jobs. Both of them had to travel clear across the city just to get to work.

A lot of shops were closed. What few that were open were generally crowded, or had long queues. The nearest barber shop was a mile away, and neither of his parents had barbering skills, so Oscar's dark brown hair had gone to seed.

Right now, he was knocking about the house looking for something to do while the power was off, and he couldn't play computer games. His device had run out of charge, and he couldn't charge it. Last time the power had stayed off three days.

He was on the ground floor, leaning on the side of the entryway to the lounge.

Something rubbed against his leg and purred.

The cat is back!

He looked down, and sure enough!

It meowed, and ran down the corridor and down the stairs to the cellar.

They always tried to keep that door closed but there was something wrong with the lock, and it always opened when there was a draught.

Where the draught came from was a mystery, as the small cellar windows were sealed glass that didn't open.

In spite of always being spooked by the door to the cellar, he followed the cat down. Something about that cat always seemed to calm his nerves.

The cat went straight to the stairwell.

'No! Not down there!'

The cat stopped at the top of the stairs and looked at him a second, as though expecting him to follow. Then it went down.

Oscar looked down the stairs. He couldn't see to the bottom, but they said it didn't lead anywhere.

He'd go quickly down, fetch the cat and come straight up.

He went down.

As he went, he could see more and more, at first, as though his eyes were adjusting to the dark, but then there was more detail than he would have expected. There appeared to be a corridor off to the right. It looked like it was daylight there.

Daylight?

At the bottom of the stairs on his left was a window. He looked out and saw he was on the third level, overlooking the row of two story terraced houses next to their house. The two windows along the corridor looked out onto the backyard, and over the roofs of the houses on the next street. Behind him was the stairs to nowhere, which seemed to be where he just came from.

Thoroughly in a daze, he followed the corridor around. It looked just like what he remembered the upstairs did when he had wandered up a year ago.

No one had ever bothered to carpet that floor, only the stairs leading up to it, and then only half way where it turned the corner, so it looked carpeted from the foot of the stairs.

He found the half carpeted stairs down to the level his bedroom was on. There was his room. He opened the door. The light was on.

Cool! The power's back on!

He forgot about the paradox for the time being, switched on the computer and played to his heart's content.

Then he started downstairs to get a snack.

On approaching the bottom step, he heard his dad asking, 'So, how was school today?'

He almost opened his mouth to say, 'It's still closed…' but someone else answered first - a kid.

'Okay, I guess.'

Why did Daddy bring a kid home?

He started around the corner and there was the kid, with his school's uniform on, just now with his back to him, taking off his jacket and hanging it on the hook. As the other kid turned into the lounge, he saw the exact image of himself.

He froze for a moment. Then he inched to the door to the lounge and peeped in carefully.

There he was, definitely himself, doing what he always did when he got home from school, watching TV.

He looked down at his own body - just checking if it was solid. He touched himself.

He inched back towards the stairs, went up and into the upstairs bathroom and looked into the mirror. Nothing wrong with his reflection.

Then, he went quietly up the half carpeted stairs to the top floor. There, he sat on the top step and put his head in his hands.

Chapter 2

Okay, this is weird.

He went over everything that had happened.

Lemme see: I went down those stairs in the cellar going after the cat, but I'm sure I came out upstairs. And then I see myself getting back from school, school isn't even open. Something's weird...

Oscar had watched enough science fiction to know that he had gone through some sort of portal. At least he had teleported from downstairs to upstairs. It had teleported him somewhere else as well.

Maybe I time travelled. Maybe that was a few days ago when school was on...

But that didn't explain the presence of his dad, who would be working late.

Maybe it's the future, and Dad loses his job?

He decided to retrace his steps back up the attic way.

As he stood up, he heard a voice downstairs, 'Dad! Why is my computer on?'

He hurried on.

Sure enough, he came up in the cellar. He went up the stairs to the ground floor. The clock in the corridor showed it was twenty minutes after he would have got home from school. He walked into the lounge.

Both his parents were there.

'Oscar! Where have you been? We've been worried sick about you!' demanded his mother.

'Three days, Oscar!' rejoined Dad. 'Where have you been these three days?'

It's the future all right!

Oscar wasn't sure whether to make up a story, or to inform them that the stairs at the top and bottom of the house were a time travel device. What could he possibly say that would be believable?

It was a while before he had the chance to say anything. By then, he thought of something that might do, even if it got him grounded.

'I was at Mike's,' he said weakly.

There was a good reason why that worked. Mike's folks were radicals, Red Bandanas, who wouldn't care that their kids' friends stayed a few days without permission. Mr. O'Gradey would have just as soon put him to work folding leaflets as send him home. In the good old days, police and social services would be all over them. Oscar was forbidden from ever going there, but at least it made a believable story.

He was grounded.

The rest of the day went on as normal, though it seemed his parents weren't working as many hours.

Then, it came out that his dad had been fired from one of his jobs. He heard his parents discussing it, and it sounded like his mother was scolding him for doing his 'usual' and that his boss wouldn't take it anymore. It sounded like *she* wouldn't take it much longer either - whatever his 'usual' was.

Oscar had never heard his mother talk to his dad that way before - like Dad was being naughty or something. It made him feel a bit uncomfortable in the stomach.

On the television news it suddenly seemed like the prospect of war was not so likely, but the Red Bandanas were more active.

The next day was apparently a school day, though Oscar wondered why he hadn't been told that sooner. So, he went to school.

For the first subject of the day, Miss Gorman told them the page number. Oscar opened to that page. They were a lot further along in that book then he thought. By jumping forward in time, he'd missed almost a whole unit.

He opened his notebook, ruled the lines in, and went to write the date.

He tapped Jennifer on the shoulder.

'What?'

'What's the date?'

'The 17th.'

Oscar remembered that yesterday was the 16th. Then it had to be a different month.

'What month?'

'April, stupid!'

It was the day after yesterday. Then he hadn't time travelled. Why was everything so different? Why were they so far along in the book? Why did his parents miss him if he was right there with them at breakfast yesterday morning?

What really confused him was that Miss Gorman talked like they'd been in class all week. School hadn't been closed! Then why was he kept home?

The next period, the whole class trooped off to the music room. This was one class he could enjoy. He and several other boys had been singled out for special voice training by Mr. O'Brian, to train their high soprano voices.

A couple of others got violin lessons, a few keyboard or guitar, one did the oboe, and the untalented just sang old Beatles and Bob Dylan songs.

Even Mr. O'Brian asked Oscar where he'd been for the last few days.

The singing was good therapy, and got his mind back to a semblance of normality. His favourite song was one Mr. O'Brian wrote himself, *For You The World Was Made.*

Megan was back from Uni when Oscar got home.

'Holidays?' asked Oscar.

'Riots,' replied Megan. 'The Red Bandanas. They're threatening to burn down the university.'

'I thought they all joined the army to fight on the border.'

'Huh? I wish they would!'

Another shock. Megan was ranting anti-war slogans the last time she was home.

'And where are *your* loyalties? *You've* been at the O'Gradey's, helping them print their leaflets, haven't you!' she accused.

'Huh? I haven't been near the place!'

'Mum said you were gone three days, and you told her you were at Mike's!'

Again Oscar was speechless. He didn't know what to tell her. He didn't know what to tell himself! Where was he for those three days? This was the 17th of April - he was here! At least time-travel would be a more believable explanation.

Oscar couldn't sleep. He went over and over the events of the day and the day before.

Changes happened every time he took the stairs. It wasn't time travel either.

But the first time he saw his future or past self. If it wasn't time travel, then that *wasn't* his future or past self but a second *present* self - or another version of himself.

Then, what about now, where his parents thought he was away?

There were those other differences. School wasn't closed, but had been in session all along. They were further along in their school work. They weren't about to go to war with 'our noble neighbours' but the problem was the Red Bandanas.

When he thought he was coming back to his own time, maybe he hadn't come back at all. Maybe another version of himself did disappear, and was still at Mike's place folding leaflets or something.

He still couldn't sleep. He got up and walked out the door.

It was cold, so he went back and put his duvet around himself, and walked out again. But instead of going downstairs, he turned right and went up to the top floor.

He stood there and looked at the stairs that went - somewhere.

Then, he thought, *Why not?*

He went up - and reached the cellar. Then he went up the stairs to the ground floor.

Now he was sleepy. He went and lay on the settee in the lounge, wrapped in his duvet, and fell asleep.

Chapter 3

His mother found him.

'Brilliant! This saves me walking all the way upstairs to fetch you. Here, I've got a clean uniform for you. I'll fetch your old one from your room later.'

Oscar followed her into the kitchen. There, he changed into a fresh pair of underwear and his uniform. He poured a bowl of cereal, and was out the door with his school bag, without even thinking about the night before.

Today was the 18th, Jessica informed him. However, for some reason, instead of going to the next chapter, they backed up to the previous chapter.

Voice training with Mr. O'Brian was the highpoint of the morning. Oscar could have forgotten all about his troubles, if not for what happened at morning recess.

A boy suddenly approached Miss Gorman, in tears, 'My mum forgot to wake me up, and I couldn't find my bag and…'

'Hey Oscar! You got a twin brother or what?' David yelled.

Oscar took a look at the one crying to the teacher, and froze.

Other children were staring at them. The other Oscar looked at him, and also froze.

Oscar suddenly knew what happened. He turned and raced out the school gate.

Half way home he stopped and caught his breath. Then he walked the rest of the way home.

He knew where the spare key was kept, so he let himself in. His parents would both be at work. He went straight to the door to the cellar.

As soon as he rounded the corner onto the carpeted portion of the stairs, he stopped short. Standing at the foot of the stairs was yet another version of himself.

'Hi,' his other self said calmly, as though he were expecting him. 'C'mon in.'

He stepped into the bedroom. Oscar followed.

'What's your name?' asked his other self.

'I-I...'

'You're new to all this, aren't you. I know, you're Oscar Wild Dougherty. We're all called that. But you gotta pick a name that *we* can tell you apart by. I got the name Percy.'

'I would have fancied a name like "Brandon".'

'I know. I would have fancied that too. So would all of us, then we'd all be called that. That wouldn't help much.'

'Has someone else got 'Brandon' yet?'

'Yeah. One of the first two that decided to do this got that. They did a rock-paper-scissors for it. The other kid got 'Blake'.'

'Uegh - that was my next choice.'

'I know. There's a way we use to pick a name. I'll show you when we get downstairs. But first, get out of that uniform. School's closed for a few days.'

Percy gave him a different set of clothes that he recognised. Oscar changed into them.

'I got another set just like that, that William wore here. I'll find a bag to put your uniform in.'

'This uniform belongs to the kid in the last place. I got in at night, slept on the settee, Mum got me up and sent me to school in these. I forgot I was in someone else's world. Anyway, during recess, he shows up crying, telling the teacher Mum forgot to wake him up, and there I was standing close by and - '

Percy was laughing.

' - and I just now ran all the way here!'

Now he was looking back on it, it did seem funny. They had a good laugh.

Then they started down stairs.

'Don't worry. Mum and Dad are at work,' said Percy.

'Is the power off here?'

'Yeah,' said Percy.

'Is Dad working two jobs?'

'Yeah, and Mum does O T. This is the world where we might go to war.'

They went straight to the cellar.

'There's a wee room down here you probably don't know about.'

They reached the bottom.

'Now, you gotta swear to keep this room a secret from all the parents, especially Uncle Milton.'

'Okay, I swear. Why especially Uncle Milton?'

'In some worlds, the prison's been broken open, and he's got away.'

'So?'

'Well, there's good news and bad news.'

'Okay?'

'He hasn't got the hots for Megan any more. She's got too big and grown up looking. That's the good news.'

'And the bad news?'

'He *does* have the hots for *us*.'

'You mean he's -'

'Yeah, and an instance of him has got through the stairs too.'

'Eugh!'

Oscar could remember that a hug by Uncle Milton often included a squeeze on the bum.

Percy led him to the darkest corner of the cellar. The dim light that came from the cellar windows on the left didn't reach far enough to see anything in the corner at the far right. Only when they came near it, could they tell there was a door.

Percy opened it. The light from the cellar window facing them showed a room only twice the size of the single bed against the far wall. It looked comfortable enough, with a bottom sheet, duvet and pillow. On the left was another door.

'That's the toilet and shower,' said Percy. 'And you can get out this window if you have to.' It was not sealed double glazed like the other cellar windows.

'Looks comfy enough,' said Oscar.

'Just wait till there's three or four of us all at once.'

'Oh. Why would there be that many of us?'

'Parents going crazy, the war, riots, Uncle Milton - we're pretty lucky actually. We have a way to escape stuff like that.'

They were sitting side by side in the bed leaning against the wall.

'You say our dad and mum go crazy?'

'How was Dad where you started out?'

'He was great! But the second place I was, he seemed to be up to stuff that got him fired from one of his jobs.'

'I bet Mum said "your usual".'

'Yup. That's what she said.'

'Yeah. In some worlds he's a great guy. In others he gets up to stuff. In some worlds it gets so weird that Mum goes over the edge. It affects some of us too. Mark can be a cry-baby, from Mum being a bit weird in his world. You gotta watch Richard. Dad, where he's from is a scumbag, and had a bad influence on him.'

Percy reached for a phone directory sitting on the little table next to the bed.

'Here. Just open it to any page, put your finger down without looking, and that's your name.'

Oscar opened it up and put his finger down. 'Margaret?'

'You can have that if you want,' laughed Percy.

'No way!'

'Then just move down until you get to a boy's name.'

'Okay - Francis.'

'Congratulations, so you're Oscar Wild Francis Daugherty!'

'Two middle names! Thats cool! Like some lord or baron or something.'

They laughed. And then Oscar Francis asked, 'Your folks okay?'

'Yeah. I didn't start here though. I just went up the stairs at the top, and couldn't find my way back. I just kept going on and on til I found these ones. They were good, but their Oscar had also got lost. They used to know about the stairs then, so they knew what happened. They let me stay in his place.'

'*Used* to know? You mean they forgot?'

'Yeah. Some grown-ups, even when they find out about the stairs, they forget. These ones forgot, and they think I've always lived with them.'

'Wow!'

'I know! If that's not weird, Timmy and Geri live with the same parents and they forgot they're not twins!'

'Woah!'

'Anyway, this room is the same wherever you go. You can always pop in and sleep if there's no place else in the house. Then you can keep looking for a new home in the morning. We call this the rats' room. '

'Why?'

'Coz we're like rats running through everyone's cellars, living off the food we find in the kitchen. Speaking of food…'

They went up to find something for lunch.

Lunch consisted of food that didn't need to be refrigerated, bread, soft butter, jam.

Oscar Francis had an idea.

'Would your folks take me as a twin?'

Oscar Percy looked thoughtful for a moment. 'Might not be a good idea -'

'Why?'

Percy was still thinking. Suddenly, he said, 'Have you met the cat?'

'We had a cat until last year. Then it disappeared. I saw it again, and it ran down these stairs out here, and that's how I got lost.'

'Grey and black?'

'Yeah.'

'There's only one of that cat. Not like everyone else. You'll meet it again.'

'How do you know?'

'It told me.'

'Huh? Like - it talks?'

'Not what you'd call talking. You'll know sooner or later. It told me you were coming. That's why I was waiting for you.'

They ate in silence for a while.

'What do I do now?' asked Francis.

'You can stay here a while. When Mum and Dad or Megan are home, we can only come out one at a time. Nothing much happens now, so no one will be asking questions you can't answer.

'But we can't just keep doing that forever,' Percy went on, 'especially if school opens up again. After a while, you should try to find another place that doesn't have one of us already living there.'

'That place I told you about, where Dad was up to something, they were missing their Oscar, and I told them I was at Mike's. They grounded me. In fact, I think I'm still grounded.'

'At least you haven't left the house, have you!'

They laughed.

'I wondered if the other one really is folding leaflets for Mr. O'Gradey. He'll really be in the soup if he is!'

'He probably found the stairs.'

'Does anyone ever get back to where they started?' asked Francis.

'There's a way you can do it. To go back to the one just before, you have to go straight back the way you came three times, and then the other way once.'

'How many worlds are there anyway!'

'Billions, probably. I don't know if all of them have this house or not. Not all of them have our family. If you keep going, you'll start finding a different family living there.

Now and then you might find a kid from a different family lost in our section.'

'Or blokes like Uncle Milton!'

'Yeah. But you can go exploring if you want, and come back here. If you take a pencil and paper with you, so you mark down where you've been, and use that to get back - like here, I'll show you…'

Percy took a piece of paper, and drew a tiny house in the upper left, '… like this. Then draw a wee arrow up or down, depending on if you went the upstairs or the downstairs way. Do that for each place you go. That way you'll know to either go up three times and down once, or down three times and up once for each place you go through.'

'Maybe I can get back to my home then.'

'Maybe, but -' he hesitated, like he did just before starting in about the cat.

'But what?'

He seemed to get fresh inspiration. 'It doesn't work as well if you go too far and spend too much time doing it. The way I told you works best if you do it the same day.'

'Oh.' Francis wondered if that was the real reason or not.

With power still off, there was nothing to do. No TV, no computer games, no smartphone or gaming devices. So they thumb wrestled, they played rock-paper-scissors, hangman, connect the dots, talked about their friends; then, because Percy missed music class, they sang.

Though they were both sopranos, they took turns singing the alto part. They sang all the songs in the repertoire. Their favourite was *For You the World was Made*, by Boz O'Brian, their own music teacher.

They had fun.

When it got dark enough to expect Mum and Dad home, Francis retired to the downstairs room with a peanut butter sandwich. Being many days without power, he was used to early nights.

He just missed his mother's goodnight kiss.

Chapter 4

The next several days were a happy time of playing, chatting, singing, and even spending time with the parents.

During the weekend, they took turns alternating between being downstairs with Oscar's parents and being in Oscar's room reading books and comics, or building something out of lego (almost like Minecraft, but actually made of physical plastic blocks). As long as one Oscar was downstairs in plain sight, no one would think of looking for Oscar in his room.

Francis enjoyed this version of his folks. They were honest, hard working, but at the same time, fun loving and lenient. Dad even had good words to say about Mr. O'Grady.

Of course, it was the world in which war with 'our noble neighbours' was an ever increasing certainty, and the Red Bandana menace was nearly forgotten.

Francis could have lived like this permanently, but they both knew he needed to find his own set of parents.

Tuesday and both parents were at work. Percy strongly suggested that Francis spend the morning exploring. With a piece of paper and a pencil in his pocket, Francis started up the upper floor stairs. Percy saw him off.

The plan was to go to just one world, and then do the back three times and once forward route taking a look at each world on the way.

He went up, and came out in the cellar.

Sunlight shone through the windows on the one wall. He went to the darkened side and found the door to the rats' room. He tried the pull-string on the light bulb.

Power was on.

There was the bed with the duvet and pillow, but no phone directory.

Francis went up the steps to the ground floor. The door was open a crack. He peeped through it and listened.

Nothing was going on. He ventured in.

Standing in the corridor he could hear something in the lounge, like snoring.

He went quietly and peeped in.

There, lying on the settee, with his back to him, his shirt not covering his whole back and his trousers not fully covering the rest, was Uncle Milton.

Oscar retreated as quickly and quietly as he could, and started up the stairs.

He had reached the top, and then realised, *No. I gotta go the other way to get back.*

'Oscar! Where have you been?' it was the whispery voice of Megan, who had just come out of her room. 'Get in here you fool!'

She pulled him into her room.

'I don't know where you disappeared to but you sure picked the worst time to get back. That creep is here!'

'I know. I just saw him.'

'And don't go into your room either! One of his mates is in there!'

'But - how...'

'Government's gone bankrupt. The whole justice system's gone belly up. Prison's cracked open. Milton moved in with a friend and Mum and Dad can't do a thing about it. It's not even safe to walk the street anymore. I don't know how you made it back.'

'I guess the Uni's closed too?'

'Yeah. Otherwise I'd take you there with me.'

'I got a place to go, actually,' said Oscar.

'Is it safe?'

'Safer than here obviously.'

'Take me with you?' asked Megan.

Oscar thought a while. 'Why not?'

'Okay, wait while I get my stuff.'

She put some things into her shoulder bag, and they were off.

Oscar led her downstairs and they tiptoed into the corridor.

'Wait,' she whispered. 'I'll get some grub.'

She took a plastic bag and started filling it with whatever she found in the fridge; bread, cheese, jam, fruit, pork pie…

Oscar heard stirring in the lounge. 'Quick! He's waking up!'

The two went into the corridor. There he stood.

'Oscar! When did you get back? I heard you -'

Oscar darted for the stairs to the cellar.

'Not down there!' screamed Megan.

'C'mon! There's a way out here!'

Megan rushed down the stairs after him. Then Uncle Milton.

Oscar made a beeline for the lower stairs, with Megan following.

'Where the hell are you -'

'C'mon! Just trust me, okay?'

She followed him down, while Uncle Milton stood at the top of the stairs, shouting, 'Ha ha! No way out down there!'

She followed him into the corridor with the wooden floor.

'What the -'

Oscar kept going. *The creep will follow us down here soon.*

Going down to the ground floor, they heard noises.1

Just ahead, in the downstairs corridor they saw Oscar backing away towards the front door. He was stark naked and wet, like he'd just stepped out of the shower.

Uncle Milton's voice came from the kitchen. 'You ain't gonna go outside like that are ye?'

Suddenly, they were aware that Uncle Milton was also at the top of the stairs.

Francis quickly grabbed the naked Oscar by the arm, saying, 'This way, Oscar!'

All three younger folk ran down into the cellar, while the two Miltons met up. They could hear their cursing as they made for the stairs to below.

Back to the top floor, they caught their breath.

'What was the scumbag doing to you?' said Megan.

'I was taking a shower, and he just walked in, grabbed me, I was soapy, so I slipped away, run downstairs into the kitchen, he comes in and chases me around the table, I crawl away under the table and into the corridor and that's where you came and - why is there another one of me? And when did you get back from Uni? And - and - why are we upstairs when we went downstairs?'

'First, let's get you some clothes,' said Francis.

They went down to the middle floor, and paused in front of Oscar's bedroom.

'Better not,' whispered Megan. 'The creep put his friend up in your room.'

'Not in all the worlds,' said Francis. 'Was anyone staying in your bedroom?' he asked the naked Oscar.

He just shook his head.

'Well, here goes,' said Francis. He knocked on the door.

They waited a minute, and went in.

The naked went straight to the chest of drawers and clothed himself.

'School's open here,' said Francis, observing the state of the desk. 'He's been doing his homework.'

'My God! You've been hopping parallel universes!' Exclaimed Megan.

They went back out and down the stairs. The house was empty. Francis led them straight to the cellar, and down the lower stairs.

In the attic again, he told the other two, 'Here, we turn around and go back the way we came.'

His sister and his dopple were still too bewildered to argue.

Coming up into the cellar, Francis immediately knew something was different. The air smelled strange. There was a layer of dust all over everything.

'We were just here. It wasn't like this!' said Megan.

'It's a different world,' said Francis, 'but it wasn't *this* different.'

He went over to the little room. The phone directory was there, but warped and wrinkled and discoloured. The duvet was all brown and looked like it would crumble if he touched it. He remembered that the little room he looked into earlier, in Megan's world, didn't have a phone directory.'

They went up to the ground floor and found even more changes. The walls were discoloured, books were blown out of their shelves, some were burnt, furniture was fallen over. Again, dust all over everything.

'What the hell happened here?' said Megan.

Francis thought he knew. 'Percy!' he cried.

'Who's Percy?' asked Megan.

'The Oscar who - *lived* - here,' said Francis. 'Called him Percy - he called me Francis.'

Megan looked through the broken glass of the lounge. 'This place has been hit by a neutron bomb!'

They walked into the kitchen.

'This was the safe place you were taking me to, wasn't it,' said Megan.

Francis only nodded, trying very hard not to cry.

'Oh Oscar,' said Megan, embracing him. 'And Percy was your friend, wasn't he.'

The other Oscar had been walking around silently, still in a daze. He was at the door to the corridor when his face suddenly lit up. 'Mummy! Daddy!'

'Oscar! This is a miracle!' Francis heard his mother say, as the previously naked Oscar ran out.

'Mummy! Uncle Milton tried to molest me!'

'Where were you when this happened?' asked Dad. 'How in the world did you survive it?'

'I was in the shower. He came in and grabbed me and started to - but I got away, and - well - Megan and - and - and that kid that looks like -'

'Well, Oscar, I'm Afraid we've lost Megan,' said Mum. 'The University was also hit, and I'm afraid -'

Megan had gone part way to the door. She looked back at Francis.

Francis, his face red and wrinkled, and tears flowing, nodded at her, and tilted his head towards the door.

'Oh Oscar!' she ran back and hugged him tight. Then she picked up her travel bag, but handed the plastic bag of food to Oscar, whispering, 'I'll remember you, Francis,' kissed him on the cheek and went out.

There were more exclamations of joy. Then Mum and Dad decided there was no point in waiting around, and left with their two children to Granddad's.

Francis took the bag of food, went slowly down the stairs to the cellar, down again to the upper floor, and quietly down the corridors and stairs, listening carefully as he went, and found the rats' room. He put the plastic bag on the small table, lay on the bed face down into the pillow, and had a good cry.

Chapter 5

As he lay there, the more he thought about it, the more he was sure there was a lot Percy didn't tell him

Why didn't he give him a straight answer when he asked if he could become his twin? That would have been super! Those few days were the happiest he'd been in a long time.

But that would have ended with *this*.

Percy also sent him on the exploration. If he hadn't he'd be dead along with Percy. Did he know this would happen?

When he said that the ways to the other world were always changing, was that the only reason for not telling him to go looking for his home world?

What if he went looking for it now?

He was hungry, and it was past lunch time. There was enough in the bag for a few meals.

There was no knife to spread it with, so he saved the bread, butter and jam for another time. He decided he'd get a knife out of the silverware drawer on the way out. He ate part of the pork pie for now.

Then he carefully went upstairs.

No one was on the ground floor, so he found a knife and put it in the bag.

There was a newspaper on the table. There were headlines about the Red Bandanas, and a bit about the disagreement over the jurisdiction over oil fields on the border.

He tried the light to see if it went on. It did.

Then he went up the stairs.

As he passed his room, he could hear voices. A couple of boys were playing, one making an aeroplane noise followed by an explosion ('Eeeeeaarrw pshkhkh!')

Francis knocked. Suddenly there was shuffling inside, and then the door opened a few inches.

The Oscar inside said, 'Woah! Where did you come from?'

'Just passing through.'

'You better keep going. There's two of us here already. We're already having a hard time keeping it quiet.'

'There's no one downstairs. I'm looking for my old home anyway. Can I come in for just a little while?'

'I guess. If you promise to move on.'

'I promise.'

The other Oscar let him in, and a third one came out from under the bed.

Toys were spread out on the floor where they were sitting, including the metal replicas of warplanes.

'Mum and Dad don't know there's two of you?'

'Nope.'

'Neither does Miss Gorman.'

'You both go to school!' asked Francis.

'Up to a couple days ago. Closed now.'

'The way I like it.'

'Take turns going?' Francis asked.

'Yeah, but it's not working very well.'

'Yeah. Hard to keep up.'

'And our friends think we're stupid coz we don't remember anything frim the day before.'

'Where you come from?' asked the one who had emerged from under the bed.

'The last place I was staying just got nuked.'

'Woah!' they both said at once.

'Just happened to be out exploring for other worlds. Kinda weird. Uncle Milton was staying in two of them.' Francis recounted the events of that morning.

They laughed at there being two Uncle Miltons being stuck together.

Then he told them about Percy.

'Percy? Oh crap!' said the one who had been under the bed.

'Who's Percy?' asked the other one.

'He's the one who told me how it all works. Had me pick my name from a phone book. Oh, my name's Louis.'

'I'm Francis.'

'See? I told you you gotta pick a name,' Louis told the other Oscar.

'Naa. I'll just be Oscar.'

'But we're all Oscar.'

'No, you be Louis, you be Francis, Percy be Percy, I'll be Oscar. Oscar Wild Daugherty.'

'Percy's dead!' sighed Louis.

'Oscar Wild was a famous writer, you know,' said just-Oscar.

'We're *all* Oscar Wild,' said Louis, exasperated. 'Be a famous writer to people *outside*. In here we gotta tell eachother apart! Especially if more of us pop by.'

'But this is my house, isn't it! I can't help it if kids keep showing up uninvited. I didn't ask for this, you know.'

'Me staying was your idea.'

'Maybe you leaving'll be my idea too,' retorted just-Oscar.

There was a heavy pause.

'C'mon Francis. Let's go downstairs,' said Louis, getting up.

'Remember, you promised to move on,' said just-Oscar.

'Don't worry. We'll move on,' said Louis.

Oscar had started saying something, but all they caught was, 'I didn't mean -' and the door shut.

Francis followed Louis down.

'He can get so-o-o annoying,' said Louis.

They went into the lounge and turned on the telly to the kid's channel. Francis settled down to Thomas the Tank Engine, and Louis came in later with two plates of chocolate cake.

Megan had her birthday already? I must have missed it for being lost.

They ate that, pretty much ignored Thomas and the fat controller, and talked about school.

The local P5 class was just ahead of Francis' home-world class, but behind the two worlds where he first lost himself. Jennifer was just as snub nosed, everything was the same.

Louis had a few choice things to say about Jennifer that shocked Francis. He laughed when Francis told him about their dopple arriving late because his mother sent Francis in his place.

Francis thought it was time to move on. Louis decided to join him.

'Looking for a place without another of us?' asked Francis.

'Or with one's just fine with me.'

'Not worried about giving him a shock? I know I would've got one.'

'Naa. They get over it. Especially when I tell them I'll do something real bad and they'll get the blame for it.'

Francis thought about the cake. *Was it Megan's birthday yet?*

'One place, I took Dad's can of spray paint and ran through the neighbourhood spraying everyone's doors and windows, shouting, "Fuck the whole world!"'

Francis got a start. To him, that was still the 'F-word'!

'That would have got him sent to juvie!' exclaimed Francis.

Louis gave a wicked laugh.

As they passed the room, Louie opened the door an inch, and said, 'I'm off. Tell Megan her cake was lovely!'

Francis thought he heard just-Oscar shout something, but they had already reached the top of the stairs.

Megan's cake wasn't digesting very well.

The trip through the next three houses went without any issue. It was midday, after all. Francis tried the lights in each place. The power was off in the first one, on in the second.

So far, Louis was sticking with Francis. *Is he trying to go home with me or what?* The last thing he wanted was a secret twin threatening trouble if he failed to please.

When they came up in the cellar of the third house, they turned right around to complete the journey.

Sure enough, it was the nuked version of their house, the top floor.

They looked out the window and saw the extent of the damage to the neighbourhood. They stood at the windows a while, taking in the scene of devastation. Some of the houses were intact, others were more heavily damaged, some had collapsed.

Francis decided to move on.

'Lemme see, I got here from upstairs, so I gotta go this way again.'

'Somebody's been here,' said Louis.

They could see that the dust had been disturbed, as though someone had been walking. There wasn't enough dust on this floor for recognisable footprints.

Francis thought about going down to look at the bedroom, but he didn't want to see what they'd certainly find. They went on upstairs.

Louis was still tagging along. Francis decided, if he did go all the way to his home world, he'd just force him to meet his parents. At least then, his parents would believe him when he explained his disappearance. Either Louis could stay as a twin, or he could move on.

The next house was where he met Megan, and they had started their escape from Uncle Milton. Just as well they weren't turning around, or they'd meet two Uncle Miltons. They went on up.

'Who the hell are you?' The voice was that of a muscular man with a full beard coming out of the kitchen, carrying a plate of leftover casserole to the lounge. He wore a tank top revealing plenty of tattoos.

Oh my God! The man staying in my room! Remembered Francis.

'Oscar,' they both said at once.

'Huh? Which one of you's Oscar?'

'We both are,' said Louis. 'Don't we look it?'

'You look like godam twins! Mil never said noth'n 'bout twins!'

He walked past them into the lounge. 'Where the hell's Mil got to anyway?'

The two dopples went quietly up the stairs, and into the next world.

As they passed the middle floor bathroom, Louis said, 'I gotta go. Wait for me.' He went into the bathroom.

Francis decided to look around downstairs.

Power was off. A newspaper in the lounge talked about the certainty of war. Other than that, nothing out of the ordinary.

He went back to the stairs, and was about to go up - and froze.

There was *Uncle Milton*!

'Well well well! If it isn't my cute little nephew, back from the wild blue yonder!' He started down the stairs.

Just then, Louis appeared behind him.

'Uncle Milton! He's not nearly as cute as me! I'm the one you want!'

Milton spun around. Then he looked back and forth between the two Oscars.

'But you gotta catch me first!' taunted Louis, as he started running towards the other stairs.

Milton started running after him.

Francis went carefully up the stairs, listening to the footsteps above. He reached the foot of the half carpeted stairs, and listened.

There was only the voice of Uncle Milton. 'That way's a dead end, you know!'

Then, half a minute later, 'Here I come!' Then footsteps up the stairs.

That *was* going to be Francis' next jump. But not if Uncle Milton was there. At least he didn't have to worry about Louis tagging along.

Oscar Francis went back to the cellar instead. He decided to call it a day, and retired to the little room. He used the knife he filched from Louis and just-Oscar's house to spread butter and cut some cheese.

His clothes were filthy from sweat and the dust from the nuke. He took them off, lay on the bed wrapped in the duvet, and thought about the day.

He had lost everything.

Why didn't he try to tag along with Megan and the other Oscar when their parents came? He was sure he could have become a twin.

Because he was too upset about Percy, that's why. Now that he thought about it, he was the only one who knew Percy was dead, and nobody would have understood why he was crying - except Megan, maybe.

He didn't mind losing Louis though. He was the opposite of Percy, the type Percy warned him about. But that was sort of heroic, what he did in the end.

He thought about Percy, and the nice parents he had. He longed for a goodnight kiss from Mum.

Now, he was no more than a rat in the cellar.

He cried himself to sleep.

Chapter 6

After waking up the next morning, Oscar stood on the bed, wrapped in the duvet and looked out the window. He could only see in an upward direction, as there was a well around the window, being that it was below ground level.

Looking up and to the left, he could still see who came and went through the front door.

Sitting down, he didn't have quite as good a view, but he could see the top of his dad's head as he went out to work, while Oscar breakfasted on bread and jam. A while later, as he stood on the bed, he saw his mother leaving for her job.

From what Uncle Milton said when he saw him, Oscer didn't live here. But just because there was a vacancy, didn't mean Oscar was going to take it. He didn't fancy living in a war zone.

Now, it was time to venture out. He took a shower, and that made him feel so much cleaner. His clothes were so smelly and dusty, he couldn't bear the thought of putting them back on. They'd just make him dirty again.

Instead of getting dressed, he picked up his clothes and ran up two flights of stairs and threw them into the hamper. The house was no stranger to his bare body. From there, he went on to his room and put on fresh clothes.

The toys hadn't been played with in a long time.

He looked for a few things that would come in useful, like a pocket knife, a flashlight, a mobile phone and charger, and a power bank. The power being off would have been why the local Oscar didn't take it along. But he could charge it in worlds he passed through that did have power, and use it where there the power was off.

He put it into his school backpack along with a few things to read, and some changes of clothes, including a school uniform, and some pajamas so he wouldn't have to sleep naked again. He also found the house key.

His backpack filled with useful items, he went back down.

He couldn't continue the search for his home-world, because Uncle Milton was in the next house on the way to it. The only way to go was down.

He'd just have to find an alternative home-world, like Percy did, and if he was lucky, it would have nice parents, and not get nuked.

And, if he was lucky, he wouldn't meet another Uncle Milton on the way.

So he set off…

Things looked okay trom the top floor corner window. He could see a bit of the street in front through that. Traffic was moderate, so things weren't real bad. The light switch worked.

He turned the corner of the corridor and froze.

A door on his left had been forced open. It was in closed position, but the part around the lock looked like it had been forced with a crowbar.

Very carefully, he turned around and went back to the stairs, and up to the cellar to the next place.

The lights worked.

He went to the top of the cellar steps and listened carefully. He could hear nothing.

He went in carefully. He peeped into the lounge, then into the dining room across the corridor. Then the kitchen. The other rooms were normally locked.

He used the downstairs toilet, and was about to go upstairs.

He heard voices. Two men were coming towards the top of the stairs. At least one of them was Uncle Milton.

If Oscar went back to the cellar now, they'd see the door close. He ran into the lounge and slipped behind the settee.

This used to be a favourite hiding spot for hide-and-seek when cousins or friends came over. The settee was set away from the wall to make room for a shelf where they put speakers and a few ornaments, which conveniently shielded him from above.

The two men walked into the Lounge.

'So, when you reckon another one will come through?'

'Can't tell. Just every few days they come. They're like rats running behind the skirting boards through a row of flats. One of them gave me the slip the other day. He just made a beeline for the nearest stairs. I was far enough behind him that he probably changed direction once he went through, so by the time I got to the other side, I didn't know if he was somewhere in that world, or had turned right around and gone to the next place.'

Both voices were Uncle Milton.

'Do Geoffrey and Marge know about it?'

'That's the funny thing. They don't have a clue!'

'What's to stop us from take'n a chair down there and just wait'n for them to come up?'

'Like fish'n? I suppose you could do that. It might take all day to get a bite. Quicker if we just went hunting for them through the network.'

'Yeah. But there's no way to get back where you started.'

'Yeah, there's that. But if we do it together, it won't matter. We'll still have each other, won't we.'

'Yeah maybe. Wanna beer?'

'Yeah. Get me one.'

One of them went out of the room, while the other turned on the TV. A football game was on.

The more Oscar heard, the more petrified he was. He hoped they wouldn't hear his heart beating.

The sound of the TV drowned that out.

The other Milton came in with the beers. 'Our supply's running low.'

'How bout we hit the newsagent for their cash and more beer, and disappear down the rabbithole ourselves on a hunting expedition?'

'Oh yeah! This would be the best get-away ever wouldn't it!'

'When you want to do it?'

'We could go right now.'

Oscar's eyes lit up.

'Naa, let's wait till this game is over.'

'Yeah, okay.'

Oscar's heart sank.

He was glad he had gone to the toilet when he did, and that the game was in the second half, because he was sure he would have wet himself before the game was over. It was long enough as it was.

At any rate, it was time enough for Oscar to come up with a plan to stop these two from preying on his dopples.

Finally, the two Uncle Miltons gathered their things and went out the front door.

On the off chance that the police were in business, he called them and told them the Newsagent on Parker Road was about to be robbed by a pair of twins with orange hair.

Robberies were one of the things the police did respond to, especially if it was a business that paid their police tax. Government revenue from other sources was no longer enough to fund the police force, thus the police tax - protection for those who could afford it.

Oscar also gave the address of the house in case they didn't catch them in time, so they could head them off.

Then he went downstairs into the little room, plugged in his phone charger, and stood on the bed at the window. This one did open, like Percy said. That way he could hear outside noises better.

He had the rest of the pork pie for lunch as he waited.

He heard sirens, and then a few gun shots from the direction of the newsagent. He waited some more.

His phone was fully charged, so he plugged the charger into his power bank, and sat on the bed and played a few games.

He was interrupted by the doorbell.

Standing on the bed, he saw a policeman standing at the door.

Better not answer it.

The policeman left after a while.

What would I tell him anyway? That they were from a parallel universe?

He went back to his gaming until he heard more noises. It was Mum. It didn't look like the happy Mum that he knew.

He waited until his dad got home, also not looking like Dad as he knew him.

He got up and went to the top of the steps to the ground floor. The door was always open a crack, as everyone had given up on trying to close it tight.

He sat next to the crack and listened.

'And what did he say?' said Mum.

'Someone they claim lives at this house, and fits the description of your brother, along with his identical twin, were arrested while fleeing the scene of a robbery.'

'You're not making any sense.'

'I didn't say it did make sense. I'm just telling you what they said.'

'How did they tell you that if Mil doesn't have a twin, and he's in prison?'

'What? Do you think I'm making this up?'

'It wouldn't be the first time.'

Nope. Not living here.

He went quietly down the stairs and into the rats' room.

After hearing his mum talk like that to his dad, it took a while for his stomach to settle, and his mind to relax.

Then he had his supper, watched some YouTube and then changed into his pajamas, and settled down for the night.

Chapter 7

Life fell into a routine. Oscar spent a day looking at each house.

He tried to be in the rats' room of each place in the morning, stand at the window and watch as first, his dad left the house, then Oscar, if he lived there, and then his mum.

He'd try to see if they were happy people or not. That wasn't always obvious, he knew, but sometimes it showed.

He would have already checked if the power was on. He realised he could also find out a lot by using the news app, whether any war was on, or if it was Red Bandanas.

Then, he'd sit next to the crack in the door and wait, in case someone like Oscar or Uncle Milton, or even Megan should wander down.

He knew about sitting still and waiting, from lying down behind the settee listening to the two Uncle Miltons.

When he was sure no one was about, he'd emerge, look around at the state of the place, and replenish his food supplies.

He really was a rat in the cellar.

Sometimes he'd watch daytime TV on the big telly. Sometimes there was something special in the fridge, and he'd help himself to a little bit. But never an uncut birthday cake. He still felt bad about that.

Sometimes he'd go out and get some fresh air. He had never before realised how nice a walk outside could be. He'd always taken that for granted.

Then, in the evening, he'd sit again by the crack in the door and listen to conversation. That told him the most about his parents.

On weekends he adjusted the routine accordingly.

Happy parents like Percy had found, or his original ones, were quite rare. Ones who didn't already have a resident son, even more so.

Which direction to go seemed to depend on what part of the house he was. If people were in the house, and he was in the cellar, it was simpler to go down, and come out upstairs. Then, to avoid meeting anyone, he had to go up to the cellar again.

Oscar wondered if he weren't missing some potentially suitable homes that way.

He decided to wait until late evening, go through the cellar to the top, and very quietly go through the house to the bottom.

Even though his parents would still be watching TV, he could go quietly from one set of stairs directly across the corridor to the stairs to the cellar.

On the second time doing this he opened the door to the rat' room, and saw there was someone in the bed already. In the dark he could see he was the right size and shape to be Oscar.

The other Oscar simply moved over against the wall and went back to sleep as Francis snuggled up next to him, as though that was the routine. Francis didn't bother to change into pajamas this time.

The next morning, the other Oscar introduced himself as Alex. He had heard of Percy, but never met him. Francis told him about that world being nuked, and his experiences saving Megan and the other Oscar from Uncle Milton.

Alex was gleeful when he heard about the two Uncle Miltons getting arrested. He had had a few close calls with an Uncle Milton himself.

Alex had already checked out this family, and was planning to go through the top floor. Francis therefore knew that no extras lived here.

Alex also had his school bag full of supplies. After he went on, Francis hung about the house, and listened to their conversation in the evening. By the sound of it, Alex was right in his assessment of them.

He took the same route to the next one.

He met more fellow 'rats' as he went; more candidates for parenthood (which he rejected); a couple near misses with Uncle Milton, though in this direction he was becoming increasingly rare.

One morning, as he stood on the bed to look out the window, he saw, instead of his dad, a man with dark skin, a woman also with dark skin, and Oscar, leaving the house together. Oscar was in his school uniform, and had a stylish haircut.

After they disappeared from sight, he heard car doors slam. Then he heard it start and drive off.

His parents didn't have a car.

After sitting by the door at his listening post, he ventured inside.

The furniture was all different, as well as the food in the fridge; and the fridge itself; and the carpet.

Oscar's old room looked like it was now the spare room. When he checked out Megan's room he could tell that was Oscar's. But it had a lot of nice things he never had. The computer was a more up to date model - a proper gaming computer. His own was a leftover office computer.

Standing up on the desk was a photo in a frame, of Oscar and the family he'd seen leaving the house with him. They looked like nice people.

They did look happy as they left the house this morning.

Oscars phone wouldn't connect to the wifi. He didn't know how to enter the password for this house's Internet router. His own data also wouldn't work.

A look at the giant screen TV showed there was neither the prospect of war, or a problem with the Red Bandanas. However, the 'billionaire politician' appeared to be the head of the opposition party, and was strongly pushing for a vote of no confidence, as the ruling party had not brought the promised recovery, nor restored key services.

Since he didn't know what sort of work hours these people had, he waited in the cellar room.

About midday, the lady of the house returned. Then, after the normal end of the school day, Oscar arrived.

Francis went up and sat next to the door and listened.

'How was school dear?'

'Okay, I guess.'

'Do you have any homework?'

'Just gotta find pictures of houses in other countries, like where it's hot or cold and stuff.'

'Okay, change out of your school clothes, I'll fix you a snack, and then I'll help you with that.'

Wow! Mum never did that for me.

Francis was sure Oscar must have come by the stairs. How else would he be here with this family?

He peeped in and saw Oscar going up the stairs, and his mum entering the kitchen.

Quietly, Francis stoll across the corridor and followed Oscar up. When he got through the door, he slipped through after him.

'Wah!' cried Oscar. Then he got a look at Francis. 'Lay off me, will ya? I don't do the stairs anymore, and I don't want no one bothering me here either!'

'Okay! Okay! Just want to know how you got this.'

'Got lost, went looking for a place, like everyone else, and came here. They're adopting me whenever social services can give them a call.'

'Good people?'

'Real good! Better than my old mum and dad were.'

'Mum and Dad couldn't afford all this.'

'No, they couldn't, but they also act a lot different. They're good, always tell the truth, don't rip people off.'

'Some versions of Mum and Dad were okay,' said Francis.

'Yeah, some.'

'What's your name? I'm Francis.'

'I *was* Robert. I won't be using that name anymore. I'll just be Oscar Wild Daugherty - or Ogbu instead of Daugherty.'

'What kind of name is that?'

'Nigerian,' said the Other Oscar.

'I'll just call you Oscar Ogbu then. Would they take one more? Tell them you had a twin?'

'They know about the stairs. They said they could only take one.'

'Social Services or something?'

'Haven't even told Social Services yet. They don't have enough people.'

Mrs Ogbu called, 'Oscar! What's taking you?'

'I'll be right there!' Oscar Ogbu called back.

He started changing quickly.

'I'll just go out the top stairs,' said Francis.

He already had his back-pack with him, so he went quickly up the stairs and into the cellar of the next house.

Oscar got to the room in the cellar just in time to see Mr. Ogbu arrive from work

He ran to the door and listened.

'How was work today dear?'

'Still the same mess. Franklin Corp still refuses to negotiate with Peabody. Flagherty is threatening to sue. I don't think Malcomb is handling the case very well.'

'Why don't you give it to Christine?'

'I might do that.'

They sounded like they got along. Oscar had no idea what they were talking about, but they sounded rich. Mr. Ogbu talked like a boss of some company.

How did Oscar Ogbu do it?

He thought probably best to step in and meet them.

He pushed the door open and stepped in. He still had on his backpack.

'Hello? What's this?' said Mr Ogbu.

'Hi' said Oscar, looking up at them. 'Can I live with you?'

'Who are you?' demanded Mr. Ogbu.

'How did you get in?' said the Mrs.

'I'm Oscar Wild Daugherty. I came up the stairs.'

'How did you get into the cellar?'

'Through the stairs at the bottom - from a parallel universe.'

Mr. Ogbu looked at Mrs. Ogbu, and said, 'The boy comes from a parallel universe.'

'Don't they all!' she replied.

'Minnie, why don't you take him into the lounge and sit with him, while I do the honours,' said Mr. Ogbu. He held up the phone as he said 'the honours'.

They're not adopting me, they're calling the police!

Oscar darted for the nearest stairway, which was the up one. In two strides, Mr Ogbu caught up with him and lifted him down by his shoulder.

'On second thought, you call. I hold him in the lounge.'

Mr Ogbu kept a firm grip on him until the police car arrived. Then he had a ride to the station.

Chapter 8

Oscar answered all their questions truthfully, so they decided he was thoroughly confused. He sat in the faux leather easychair, alone in the room, waiting for someone from Social Services to fetch him.

Social Services wasn't what it used to be, which was why it was such an easy matter for Robert to settle in with a family. That was also why they might just have to put him into a cell for the night if they didn't have anyone to send.

They'd even called the Ogbu family to ask if they were sure they didn't want to take him in.

They had examined all his stuff, and even checked the number on the phone. The number wasn't in service in this world.

So Oscar sat hugging his backpack. He would have played some games on his device, but his mind was too unsettled for that.

What's gonna happen to me now?

Even if he escaped from wherever they'd be taking him, he was sure he'd never find his way back home again.

Whatever that house was, it was home - even to the rats in the cellar.

He wanted to cry.

Something rubbed against his feet and purred.

The cat!

In fact, it was the very same grey and black cat.

'How did you get in here?'

The cat started to walk away, then looked back and meowed.

'I donno. Last time I went after you, look where it got me.'

As though answering him, it ran and jumped up onto the back of the soft seat, lay down and purred loudly in his ear.

Oscar imagined he could see himself following the cat down the cellar steps that day. He felt like he was simply imagining it, but his imagination was on autoplay. He saw the cat stop at the top of those stairs and look at him, inviting him to follow. He saw himself hesitate at the top of the stairs, and then go after the cat and disappear into the darkness. Then, all he could see was the empty cellar.

Suddenly, it went all white - so white that even though it was his imagination, it blinded him. Then it was full of smoke. That cleared, leaving it looking just like the cellar of Percy's house after it was nuked.

The purring died down.

'Oh my God! You saved my life!'

He was breathing heavily. Soon, his breathing relaxed.

'But - but why couldn't you save Percy like that?'

The cat began purring again.

Now Oscar saw himself and Louis having arrived at the top floor of Percy's house. Louis saw the signs that someone had been down the corridor.

This time, instead of hurrying up the stairs, he went down to the middle floor. He hesitated in front of the bedroom door, preparing himself for what he was sure he'd see.

They went in. No remains anywhere. But he looked on the desk.

In the dust, a finger had scrawled, 'I'm still alive. Follow the cat.'

Outside the door again, they saw cat's paw prints going down the corridor towards the downstairs.

'He really did know you. You really did talk to him!'

Now the cat purred in a more relaxed way, like a cat being stroked.

Then, it jumped to the floor and walked again to the door. This time, Oscar followed.

The police lady probably hadn't meant to leave the door slightly ajar. No one looked up as Oscar followed the cat along one side of the main room with all the desks with policemen entering reports and fingerprinting suspects. Nor was it likely that the side door was supposed to be open.

At any rate, Oscar soon found himself out in the back alley with the cat leading him towards what didn't look like a way out.

In fact, it was a dead end - in fact so dead an end, no tramp in his right mind would even sleep there - even if not in their right mind, as is sometimes the case.

But apparently, dogs were a different matter. A dog about the size of Oscar began growling at them, threatening to devour them if they stepped any farther.

Oscar froze.

But the cat simply stood, lifting a forepaw with claws extended. The dog stood there looking at the cat.

Then the cat hissed, and the dog turned and ran squealing out of the alley. The cat quietly led on.

Behind some rubbish bins, was what looked like a door. Really, it was a patch of intense blackness in the shape of a door that was hard to distinguish between a physical door and empty space.

The cat walked right in, and so did Oscar.

The light of the sky suddenly blinded him, as salt spray hit his face driven by the wind behind the wave that had just crashed on the rocks. Looking behind him he saw it as if he had just emerged from a lighthouse. The cat jumped from rock to rock, down to the shore line.

The water from the last wave was still dribbling down before the mouth of a cave. Oscar hurried in after the cat, expecting to be drenched by the next wave.

Instead, it was suddenly pitch black. The air was warm and humid. When his eyes adjusted, he seemed to be in a room with long strings hanging between racks, like noodles hung out to dry.

The cat was walking towards a partly open doorway. Oscar followed.

They came out into a half enclosed room full of tubs and contraptions that probably had a very specific use.

A Chinese boy in an undershirt and shorts was staring at him from behind a vat.

'Mama! Why a guailo boy in the noodle room?' he called.

Oscar followed the cat onward, as he heard a woman answer partly in what was probably Chinese, part English. 'You finish [something something] first and then you [something something] about guailo boys, ah?'

Now, they were walking through what appeared to be a dense, half outdoor market, shaded by canopies and giant umbrellas, and the eaves of a row of shops on the right, and everywhere tables and glass cases with every type of food, mostly Asian, and people selling. A jumbled sound of selling, haggling and other conversation was happening in Chinese (or whatever it was) with generous amounts of English thrown in. 'Cost too much la!' Just beyond the tables and canopies on the left, he could make out motorbikes, bicycles, three wheel taxis and push carts all trying to get around each other.

Suddenly, the cat stopped, sat down, looked up at a table, and meowed.

A very old man looked over the table. 'Ah! My old friend! This time you bring a boy with you!' He looked at Oscar. 'You hungry, ah? Here, just wait.'

He disappeared into the back, and returned with a plate with a fried fish, which he set on the ground for the cat. Then he gave Oscar a large steamed roll. 'And *chasil pao* for you.'

The cat gave a sort of 'thank you' sounding meow.

'Thank you sir,' said Oscar.

'I thank the cat,' said the man.

Oscar bit into the roll. It was a soft, fluffy bread with delicious pork in a red gravy inside. He was very hungry, as they hadn't got around to feeding him at the police station.

'You take good care of the cat, ah? He take care of you. Very wise cat. Very old. He save my life when - when I was your age.'

The cat was finished, and meowed to the man, and started walking.

Oscar was on his last bite.

The cat stood in front of a manhole cover and meowed again.

'Ah! You go out this way this time.'

He got out an iron bar with two bent prongs on the end. He used it to pick up the cover by the holes on the middle and lifted it up. The cat jumped into the darkness below.

The man looked at Oscar. 'You better follow the cat. Don't worry, you won't hurt yourself.'

Oscar went to the hole and hesitated.

'I help you down, ah?'

The man picked Oscar up, and lowered him carefully down the hole. As soon as Oscar could see the ground under him, the man let him go.

He was standing under a bridge over a canal. The air was suddenly cooler. It wasn't dark at all, though it looked so from the street above. A hole in the concrete above him closed with a clang as he looked up at it, leaving no sign of a hole.

Along the bank, but under the shelter of the bridge were people, some families, some with children, huddled in groups, some with gas camper cookers, some with open fires, all looking like they lived there.

'Where did *you* come from?' asked a woman in what sounded like an American accent.

He heard the meow of the cat and saw it sitting just beyond the shelter of the bridge. He followed it onward

'He's with the cat,' he heard someone say.

They walked parallel to the road on their right, until it came down to their level. They stopped before they came to a wall supporting an overhead bridge. The road curved left at that point. It was a blind curve, and the traffic was heavy. The cat seemed to be waiting for a break.

It came, and the cat darted out. Oscar simply ran after the cat, suddenly feeling like he could be hit any time - as he couldn't actually see to his left before crossing.

Not a safe thing to do unless accompanied by a wise cat.

They came to an island in the middle of the dual carriageway, and walked down the middle - heavy traffic on both sides - until they came to a utility box.

There was an opening at the bottom, where the cat went in. Oscar had to get on his hands and knees, and take off his backpack and push it in front of him.

They came out in the familiar cellar, from under the stairs leading up to the ground floor.

Or rather, Oscar did. He couldn't find the cat anywhere. But he was home.

Chapter 9

Inside the rats' room, he settled on the bed and tried to make sense of the day's events.

He knew it really happened, because when he burped, the taste of the delicious red pork came up.

He was tired from all the stress, the walking, the strange places, he was sweaty from the warm humid climate.

He took a shower, put on his pajamas and went to bed. He fell asleep quickly.

In the middle of the night he woke up. The cat was purring next to his ear. The relaxing purr put him back to sleep again.

He dreamed that he could also purr. He was purring for his young cousins who were living through a family crisis.

In the morning the cat was gone.

He hadn't had a chance to top up his food supply, so he had to wait until he could explore the house.

There was no power, but there was still charge in his phone, and his number was in service. The news app told him the Red Bandanas were active, and a demonstration in the city centre had gone violent.

He watched his father, and then his mother leave the house. But his mother seemed to be later than usual.

He went and sat next to the door to listen.

There were voices - children's voices, coming from the kitchen.

One of them screamed. Another shouted at someone, either for screaming, or making the first one scream.

It was his cousins. No grown up seemed to be about. Nor Oscar, apparently. If he was home, it would have been his job to mind them.

He stepped into the ground floor space and into the kitchen.

'Oscar, Becky won't let me have Cheerios!' said Alan, as soon as he saw him.

'Coz he makes a mess every time, and I ain't clean'n that!' said Becky, the oldest (two years younger than Oscar).

Oscar went immediately around to where Alan was and scooped Cheerios off the table top and into Alan's bowl, and poured him some more from the box. The floor could be cleaned later. They were eating their cereal dry, as milk would go off without electricity.

'Auntie Marge said you were gone,' said Becky.

'I'm only back for a little while,' said Oscar, fetching himself a bowl and pouring Cheerios.

The youngest two, Mickey and Lydia were eating quietly, until Lydia decided to start talking.

'Mummy tried to kill Daddy,' Lydia was the youngest, at four years old.

Alan added, 'Daddy punched Mummy in the nose, got blood everywhere…'

'Shut up!' said Becky.

'… and then Mummy went after Daddy with a knife, and then the police came, and then Auntie Marge came and fetched us.'

Mickey, the five-year-old piped up, 'Mummy's gonna go to prison, just like Uncle Milton!'

'No, she's not!' screamed Becky.

At least that meant Uncle Milton wasn't on the loose.

They ate in silence for a while - except Becky.
Oscar noticed she was sobbing.
'It'll be okay, Beckey.'
'No it won't. You're just say'n that!'
She was right. It did sound hollow. How did he know it would be alright?

As they had finished breakfast, Oscar gathered the bowls into the sink, and put the cereal away, and cleaned off the table, and swept up the cereal on the floor.

Then he followed the younger ones into the lounge.

Mickey and Alan were already fighting over the toys. Lydia was jumping up and down on the settee. Becky was curled up in a corner of the settee, moping.

Suddenly, Lydia stopped jumping, and said, 'Oscar, I went peepee on myself.' She was all wet on her lower half.

Oscar sighed. 'Where's the suitcase?'

Beckey pointed to a bag in the corner. Oscar opened it, picked out a pair of shorts her size, and led her by the hand to the toilet.

He had done this a few times before. Because of this family, he knew the basic differences between boys and girls.

He left the wet trousers in the sink, and they went back to the lounge, where Mickey was crying that Allan had hit him and Beckey was still giving the world the silent treatment.

Oscar wondered how Mum expected the kids to survive all by themselves. On the other hand he did know her boss was unrelenting.

He sorted Alan and Mickey out by taking away the offending toy, a flexible Noddy figurine, and putting it on a high shelf where they couldn't reach it, and pulling out more toys from the toy box Mum had brought down from his room.

Lydia was back to jumping up and down on the settee.

Mickey still wanted the ones Alan had, and Alan didn't believe in compromise.

Oscar said, 'Lydia, stop jumping like that. You're gonna break the springs.' He grabbed her to get her down.

Lydia suddenly started crying, 'I want Mummy!'

Now, Becky had her hand over her ears, obscuring her face with her elbows, with her eyes tightly shut.

Oscar stood there and looked, feeling helpless.

No wonder their mum went crazy!

But their parents acting like that probably made them worse.

He remembered he had dreamt about these cousins, and that they settled down when he purred like the cat.

How the heck do I purr?

Purring came naturally to a cat, but not to a boy.

What did come naturally?

He started singing.

It was his favourite of all the songs Mr O'Brian had taught them. He had sung it with Percy ...

Blessed are the poor, the blind,
the lame, the trodden down
With the poor and contrite spirit,
there I will be found
Yours is the Kingdom of Heaven,
do not be afraid
The earth is your inheritance,
for you the world was made

As he got into the first stanza he did feel like it was coming up as a cat's purr would. It even felt like it was last night's purring that had so soothed him, that was now coming out through his high soprano voice.

Blessed are those that mourn,
for I will comfort you
Those who come weeping,
praying as I bring you through
I will lead by streams of water,
along smooth paths I've laid
The earth is your inheritance,
for you the world was made

Lydia had stopped crying, and was looking up at him. Becky's eyes were open, and looked soft. The boys were no longer fighting, and were just listening.

Oscar paused.

'Sing some more,' said Mickey.

All their faces seemed to agree.

He started the third stanza.

Blessed are the meek, whose only
hope is in the Lord
When evildoers are cut off,
the wicked are no more
You will inherit the land,
in peace that will not fade
The earth is your inheritance,
for you the world was made

Blessed are you who hunger now
for things that ought to be
Thirst for justice, mercy served,
the oppressed set free
You will see your dream come true,
your hunger will be stayed
The earth is your inheritance,
for you the world was made

As he sang, he knew that so much of it might have sounded like a pipe dream, what with all that was happening, the war, the riots, the actual hunger and poverty, even the state of these kids. But this wasn't the hollow sounding 'It'll be okay' that he told Beckey earlier. Somehow, as he sang, he knew each word was meant to be.

He finished all the stanzas, and they all simply looked at him for more.

He sat on the settee as he started singing it through again. Lydia and Mickey snuggled up on each side of him. Allan sat cross legged on the floor with his chin resting on his hands. Becky just sat where she was, but looked more reconciled with the world.

After that, the children went back to what they were doing, but peacefully. Oscar got Noddy back down, and Lydia played with that.

For lunch, Oscar made peanut butter sandwiches. He made a couple extra for himself for later.

Before his mother was due back, he slipped out quietly. His cousins were playing, reading and napping contentedly.

With his backpack, he went up through the upstairs.

Chapter 10

Oscar thought it would be better to make his way back here, exploring the worlds on the way, and then check up on his cousins on his return, rather than stay around while his young cousins were telling his parents about him.

He arrived in the cellar, and checked the lights. Off. He checked the news app. A different neighbourhood not far from here had been nuked a few days ago. Things were in chaos.

Not a safe world to stay in.

He went down cellar steps to begin his return journey to check up on his cousins.

The upstairs light switch came on. He went and sat on the half carpeted stairs just out sight of his bedroom door, and peeled his ears.

While there, he checked the news app. There was a dispute with 'our noble neighbour' that looked like, couldn't be resolved, and no one was making any moves to offer a compromise, no matter what the pro peace people said.

I know what Megan will rant about in this one.

He also knew staying could be fatal.

Half way down the stairs to the ground floor, suddenly there, appearing in front of him, was Uncle Milton. Before he could think to turn around and flee, his uncle was already towering above him. He had as much chance of escaping up the stairs now with his short legs as he did from Mr. Ogbu.

'Ha ha! Finally caught me one!'

Oscar just froze.

There was a hiss behind him.

'Oh God, I swear I'll kill that cat!'

Oscar was only looking straight ahead, at Uncle Milton. But he heard a long low meow.

Instinctively, Oscar stiffened his neck in response.

The cat took a leap, ricocheted off Oscar's head and on to Uncle Milton's face, causing him to fall backwards.

Next thing Oscar knew, Uncle Milton was sprawling, head downward on the stairs.

Oscar just stood there and looked.

'Oh my God, I can't move! Get that cat away from me!'

Oscar wasn't about to stop the cat from anything.

'Call emergency! And for @#&* sake get that cat off me!'

The cat was sitting next to his ear, purring. It looked up at Oscar and meowed.

Oscar knew that meant, call emergency, not get the cat off him, nor the dirty word he had uttered.

Oscar called emergency.

Then he stepped carefully around Uncle Milton, and went to wait at the door.

Uncle Milton soon stopped cursing, and started crying. The cat kept purring.

As soon as he heard the siren, Oscar opened the door. The medics came in and began examining Uncle Milton.

The cat moved a distance away, while they asked Uncle Milton what he could feel when they pricked him. He couldn't feel anything.

Then they brought in a gurney, and very carefully got him on to it.

The cat jumped up next to his head and began purring some more. One of the medics started to pick up the cat.

'I think the cat needs to go with him,' said Oscar.

They let it stay.

As they wheeled him out the door, Uncle Milton said, 'Oscar, I'm really really sorry okay? Tell the other Oscars I'm sorry. I've been horrible to you all!'

The cat turned to Oscar and meowed.

A medic asked him, 'Will you be okay?'

Oscar nodded.

Oscar automatically started walking down to the cellar, and then down to the top floor of the next house.

He was already halfway to the cellar before he realised that the cat's last meow had sent him that way - just as the cat's meow had made him stiffen his neck before it used his head as a jumping post.

He was understanding the cat, just like Percy did.

As soon as he got into the rats' room, his mother arrived upstairs - probably the same time as Mum was arriving in the house where Uncle Milton fell down the stairs - and Mum was arriving home to his cousins to find the house not torn apart.

The lights were off, and riots were happening in various places.

After his dad got home, he went to his listening post.

Oscar still lived there. He had been to school in spite of there being no power. Dad and Mum seemed like okay people.

Since Dad and Mum charged their phones at work where they had solar panels, they could receive calls. Mum got a call, apparently from Aunt Maggie.

He heard her say, 'Okay, but I can't just keep bailing you out like this! You know we've both got jobs. Oscar can't help this time as he's just started back to school.' Then, after a pause, 'Alright, I'll go fetch them. This will be the last time, and I'll send you the bill for any damage they cause.'

'Those brats again?' he heard Dad say.

'Yeah. Maggie's been arrested for assault, and Joe is dead drunk. I'll go fetch them now.'

Oscar went back to the room.

This wasn't a prospect for a home, but he'd pitch in.

A while later, he saw his mother returning. She was holding Lydia, and he saw the tops of the heads of the other three.

He played games on his device, using up the charge in the phone itself. Then he put it on charge from the power bank.

He had one of the peanut butter sandwiches for his supper.

As he did the previous day, Oscar made his entry as his young cousins were at breakfast, this time, wearing his school uniform. This day started more positively, as Oscar was focused on what he was there for.

After he arbitrated the usual disputes, he sang for them. It had the same effect as the day before.

After lunch, he made himself a cheese sandwich for evening, and a jam sandwich for breakfast.

He told the kids he was popping out and would be right back. The Oscar returning from school would deliver on that promise.

In the morning, Oscar made the final two steps to where he had left his first group of cousins, by going through the cellar to the top floor, and there, turning around and coming up the cellar again.

He waited till he saw his mum leave the house, and went up into the ground floor. He could already hear the kids in the lounge. He stepped in - and his heart stopped.

There, sitting on the settee, holding Lydia and Mickey on either knee, and Alan and Becky snuggled up on either side, was *Uncle Milton*.

'Oscar, how lovely to see you!'

Oscar was about to scream at his cousins to get away from the pervert, when suddenly the cat pranced in passed him, and jumped on to the back of the settee and purred at the back of his head.

'And you, my dear furry friend.'

Oscar stood there, thoroughly confused.

Uncle Milton's expression slowly changed from jovial to a more subdued, concerned look.

'Oscar, I have a lot to tell you. First I'm sorry for what other instances of me have done to you, and the other instances of you. Can you forgive us?'

Oscar didn't know what to say. He thought about the Oscar who was running away naked.

The cat meowed and looked at him.

Oscar still wasn't sure..

'I don't know. It's just not something that should be done to kids.'

'You're right. It's not. That last one of me you met, the cat was just telling me about it, got what was coming to him. He got what we all deserve. But you know, if you hadn't called emergency services, he'd be dead by now. And he'd have deserved that too.'

'The cat told me to.'

'Yes, he did, because you cooperated, the cat was able to help him in the same way he has helped me. He's totally paralised, but something's come to life on the inside, and, in a way, he's more alive now than before.'

There was a long pause.

Becky spoke up. 'Forgive him, Oscar, like in the song you sang.'

'The song I sang? That wasn't about forgiving, that was about -'

'Of course it was! When you sang it, we forgave each other.'

'I forgived Mummy and Daddy,' said Mickey.

'Me too,' said Alan.

Oscar decided he'd forgive all the Uncle Miltons.

He sat down on the other end of the settee. 'When did you get out, Uncle Milton?'

'I've been out for a few months now, on good behavior. They saw such a change in me. But that was in a different world. The cat brought me to this one. The local Uncle Milton is still inside.'

'How did you change?'

Uncle Milton thought a while. 'Some of the most beautiful things in the world can also become the most ugly,' he began, 'and some of the strongest things can either do the most good, or be the most destructive - like nuclear power. Nuclear power comes from the smallest parts of what makes things exist. You can use it to make electricity to turn on the lights, to run everything in the house, charge your phone, keep the food fresh, cook the food; or if you use it the wrong way - well, I think you've seen what a nuke can do.'

'Yeah,' said Oscar.

'One of the most powerful and beautiful things,' he went on, 'is love. I was given a great capacity to love, but I used it the wrong way. I saw the beauty in people, and I loved that beauty. But I didn't practice loving the right kind of beauty.

'You see, people are the most beautiful when you enjoy the whole person. You begin by loving their personality, their friendship, their thinking mind, and sharing your friendship and your thoughts with them, that's where love begins to grow to be a beautiful thing. That's friendship.

'There's other kinds of love, beginning with love between friends, and there's love that your mum and dad have for each other, and love that your mum and dad have for their kids, and kids have for their parents. And there's the kind of love you have for people who are suffering and poor, and you feel like you want to help them.

'Well, me? I never learned the first kind of love. I started seeing the beauty of people's bodies before I learned to appreciate their souls. I fed my mind on that until it became something you can't even call love anymore.

'That's what made all your Uncle Miltons become some of the worst and ugliest specimens of humanity, so that you Oscars aren't sure which is worse, having Uncle Oscar around, or having a nuke land in your neighbourhood.

'But this cat's purring has been healing me, and opening my mind to the right way. But, the cat tells me you also purr.'

'Sing to us Oscar,' said Alan.

'Yeah!' said the others at once.

So, Oscar sang for them again. This time, he felt it coming from even deeper.

Chapter 11

Oscar would never have believed he could have had such a good time with Uncle Oscar and his young cousins, but he did.

They took a walk to the newsagent, the same one the two Uncle Miltons tried to rob in the other world. This Uncle Milton bought sausage rolls, a treat Oscar hadn't enjoyed in a long time. He bought a few more pastries for Oscar to take away for his supper. The shop had a generator, so they could keep them warm in the glass case during blackout.

On the way home, Uncle Milton said to Oscar in a low voice, 'Only tell the Oscars that you trust, but my unique name is Benjamin. None of the other Miltons know that. That's in case we meet again, so you know it's me.'

Oscar told him his name was Francis.

Then, Uncle Milton stuck a few folded up bank notes into Oscar's shirt pocket, and said, 'That's for when you need it,' he said.

'Thank you, Uncle Milton.'

Mid afternoon, he went off via the upstairs route, planning to visit the other set of cousins the next day.

He entered the world in which Uncle Oscar had fallen down the stairs, and thought he would settle down in the rats' room for that night.

But this is where they've been dropping nukes!

He went to the linen press, ferched himself a spare duvet and a pillow, went down through the cellar to the top floor of the house his young cousins were in. He spread the duvet next to the half carpeted stairs and camped there for the rest of the day and that night.

He could hear their voices from time to time, but they seemed to be doing okay. He also heard Oscar and his parents whenever they went in and out of their rooms.

As their bedroom door was closing, he thought he heard his dad say, 'They seem to be very well behaved this...'

He had the ham and cheese pastries that Uncle Milton had got him, for his supper.

The next day, after the local Oscar and both parents had left the house, Oscar wandered down.

Again, they were at breakfast, but there were no major spills to be cleaned up. Oscar poured himself some Cheerios, and joined them.

Mickey asked him, 'Are you Percy, or Francis?'

Oscar almost spilled his own Cheerios.

Beckey rephrased the question, 'Did you just come yesterday, or the day before?'

'Did one of me come yesterday?'

'Yeah. But he said he didn't come the day before.'

Alan said, 'But Oscar who lives here says he didn't sing to us at all! He thinks we're just be'n silly!'

'But Oscar that came yesterday says his name is Percy, and he thinks you might be Francis,' finished Becky.

Oscar Francis replied, 'I am Francis. I lost Percy and thought he was dead because something horrible happened to the house where he lived, but somebody told me he got away. I would like to find him again.'

Breakfast was finished. Oscar put away the dishes and cleaned the table, and went into the lounge. As soon as he sat down, Lydia clambered onto his lap.

'Sing for us!' she said.

'Yeah!' said Mickey and Alan together.

So he began singing *For You The World Was Made*.

About the third stanza he was sure he heard a second voice singing the alto part. On the fourth stanza he was positive.

Beginning the fifth, another Oscar appeared in the door from the corridor. The younger ones were beside themselves.

They finished that stanza, and Francis and Percy were in eachothers arms.

Soon they were sitting, each with one of the youngest on their lap, Alan wedged between them and Beckey next to Percy, catching up on each other's adventures.

Francis learned that had he found Percy's message scrawled on his tabletop, and followed the cat's paw prints, he would have caught up with Percy long ago. Because he hadn't, his adventures were much more interesting than Percy's.

Percy was relieved that the parents of that world weren't bereaved - though only Francis, Percy and the other Megan, knew that the Megan of that world did in fact perish. He was amused to hear of the two Uncle Miltons' attempt to rob the newsagent, and fascinated by Francis' trip around the world. However hearing of the reformed Uncle Milton wasn't a surprise. The cat had been filling him in.

During lunch, the lights suddenly came on. When they got back to the lounge, they decided to turn on the telly.

Francis was about to switch from the news channel it was on, to one of the kiddy channels, but something made him stop.

There, on the presenters' desk, purring into the microphone, was their cat.

'Look! A pussycat!' said Mickey.

'That's *our* cat,' said Percy.

The presenters were making jokes about the sudden arrival of the cat.

Francis recognised the purring as more than a contented cat's purr. It had purred like that in his own ears at the police station, in bed telling him he could purr, even long time ago whenever his nerves needed to be calmed. It had purred like that for Uncle Milton after he broke his neck.

A studio hand picked the cat off the table and took it away. The presenters went back to their script.

A minute later, the cat jumped into the desk and started purring again.

The studio hand said, 'We took it outside, we locked it in a room, how does it keep coming back?'

Again, he took it away. Again…

'I like that cat. Let's watch this!' said Alan. The other children agreed.

They spent the afternoon hearing their cat purr to the nation as the news team tried to maintain a semblance of a newscast.

After that, Francis and Percy went together up the stairs to the next cellar. Francis thought the local Oscar would *really* think the kids were being silly now.

Francis and Percy settled into the rats' room and got out their smartphones.

When Percy was warned to leave his place before it got nuked, he had also packed his school bag with all the same things Francis had in his.

They checked the news app and found that in this world, war looked inevitable. However the leaders were still talking.

When they saw their father had returned, they both went and sat by the door at the top of the stirs.

Oscar didn't live here.

'But they're not very happy though,' observed Francis. 'Both at each other a lot.'

'But sometimes, they're only like that coz they've lost their kid,' whispered Percy. 'They just aren't happy any more after that. You got to listen for other stuff, like does Mum think Dad is being a crook, or a liar, or if they say something that hurts really deep. So far I don't hear anything about that.'

They walked back to the room.

'If they're just in a bad mood all the time, they'll suddenly be happy again if one of us shows up,' said Percy.

'But we might be in trouble though.'

'Not if you've been away long enough. They'll just be so happy having you back they forget to get angry.'

'Do you think this is a good family then? What if we both go in together and they take us as twins?'

'Maybe - but -'

There, he's doing it again!

But Percy added, 'I think there's something important we gotta do first.'

Chapter 12

As they were turning in for the night, the door opened, and there was another of them.

'Hi. Room for one more?' he said, when he noticed there were two already. He sounded a bit nervous.

'Sure, as long as you don't mind being a bit cramped,' said Percy. 'Do you mind, Frances?'

'I guess not.'

'I'm Percy. What's your name?'

'Oh, hi Percy! It's me, William!'

'Wow cool! Where have you been?'

'Well,' he hesitated, and his expression changed, 'I found a great place, Mum and Dad were real good, and I thought I had it made, but -'

'But what?'

'Uncle Milton, two of them!'

'Yeah,' said Francis. 'They've started hunting in pairs.'

'Yeah, Mum and Dad went to a wedding, so I was by myself, and well, they musta heard me in the shower, and they came in. They caught me, but one of them slipped, and I got out. Then I ran for the upstairs, but I heard them come'n after me, so I went up to the cellar, and turned around, and back and forth like that, but I lost count how many times, then I came out upstairs, and ran down to the cellar again, and - well - the whole family was there just come'n out of the kitchen, Oscar, Megan, Mum, and I dash passed them naked - I don't know what they thought - but I got down the stairs in the cellar, and back to the top. And I just popped into the bedroom, and no one's there, so I put on some clothes, went back up, and - well - here I am.'

'Woah!' said Percy.

'Wow!' said Francis.

'You should be safe now, anyway,' said Percy.

'You're still wet,' observed Francis.

'Yeah. And I'm lost.'

'No, you're not,' said Percy. 'We've found you. I think we're supposed to do something together.'

'Like what?' asked Francis.

'Don't know yet.'

They snuggled up for the night.

In middle of the night, Francis heard purring.

Then he heard a whisper, 'There's a cat in here.'

And then, 'It's okay. He's a friend.'

He went back to sleep.

For breakfast they shared two jam sandwiches three ways.

'Where did that cat go?' William asked. 'How did it get in here anyway?'

'That cat goes through portals we don't know about,' said Francis.

'Yeah! It took you to China didn't it,' said Percy.

'It's weird,' said William. 'Last week where I was, the Red Bandana people were having talks with the Prime Minister and other bigshots, and when they come out to talk to the cameras, a cat jumps up on the table, and starts purring, and they say that in the meeting, that cat got in and was going around purring at everyone, and it put them in such a good mood that they made an agreement.'

'That would be the same cat that was in here last night,' said Percy.

'We saw it in the news yesterday,' said Francis, and they told him...

'But that cat can sure purr, can't it!' said William. 'It put me right to sleep, and then I dreamt that we were all purring together, all three of us, and also a whole bunch more of us.'

'I dreamt I could purr,' said Francis. 'The next day I went upstairs and found Becky, Allan, Mickey and Lydia, and they were all by themselves, acting real wild, and I thought about that dream, so I sang to them.'

The three decided that they weren't looking for a home right now, and since they didn't know for sure what they were supposed to be doing, they stayed put.

After the house was empty, they went up to the ground floor. At first, they just sat in the lounge. Later, they looked in the bedroom.

Since the Oscar from this room was lost in the parallel worlds, Percy suggested that William help himself to the school bag, and fill it up with a few changes of clothes, and the smart phone and charger.

So, William was a fully kitted cellar rat.

They watched the news, and the report on the talks between the two nations over their border dispute revealed that their cat had been up to more mischief. The talks had suddenly started going somewhere.

For lunch, they helped themselves to some leftover stew from the fridge which they microwaved.

'The only thing is,' said Percy, 'We can't just keep eating here. They'll run out of food, like they're supporting three kids when they don't have any.'

Francis remembered the cash Uncle Milton (Benjamin) had given him. 'We can go to the newsagent's and buy some. I got a bit of cash here.'

So they took a walk and came back with a loaf of bread, a tub of butter, a block of cheese, and a jar each of jam and peanut butter.

It was still early afternoon, an hour yet before Mum was due back, so they were still sitting in the lounge.

Another Oscar wandered in.

'Hi! Did I miss anything?'

'We don't know yet. Stick around and find out.'

'I'm Louis, by the way.'

'Hi Louis,' said Francis. 'Me, Francis. That's Percy. He didn't die after all. And that's William. Oh, and thanks for getting Uncle Milton off my tail.'

'Oh yeah, I got him *lost*!'

Before they went back down, the boys got an extra duvet and a few pillows out of the linen press.

Francis and Percy slept with the extra duvet on the floor while William and Louis slept on the bed.

In the middle of the night, Francis was awakened by Louis' voice, 'Oh my God, there's a *cat* in here!'

Then he heard the purr.

'Here cat you don't belong - *OW*!' And a little later. 'C'mon, cat you get - *HOY! That hurt!*'

There was a low angry meow, and then more purring.

'I think the cat's gonna stay put, Louis,' said Percy.

'Well, if the cat's not going anywhere, I'll just -' there was some shuffling, and a hiss and another angry meow. Then a whimper, 'Aw *c'mon*!'

And now Louis's staying put, thought Francis.

Now, just purring.

After a while Francis thought he heard sobbing.

Nobody made any comment on the scratches on Louis' face and hand the next morning, though Francis imagined one was for Megan's birthday cake, and the other for spray painting the neighbourhood.

They breakfasted on what they bought from the newsagent the day before, and then went to hang out upstairs.

They watched daytime TV and talked about things, mostly about their experiences in the network of worlds.

Louis was mostly quiet.

Percy suggested singing, so they sang a few rounds of Boz O'Brian's *For You The World Was Made.* Since that song not only had soprano and alto but also descant, and in some bars, a fourth part, they were able to give it the full works.

They went on to other songs in their repertoire, but kept coming back to that one. There was something about that song.

When they were all sung out, they just sat in silence. Francis was amazed how good it felt, like when singing to his cousins.

Louis broke the silence, 'I felt like we were purring like the cat.'

After a long pause, William said, 'We were.'

They were still mulling it over, when suddenly three more Oscars stumbled in.

'Did a cat come through here?' Said one of them.

'We're supposed to be following it,' said another. 'Now it's disappeared.'

'It was probably bringing you here,' said Percy. 'I think we're here for a reason.'

'You're just in time for lunch though,' said Francis.

They gathered around the kitchen table and made themselves cheese on toast. They finished off the bread and the cheese.

The newcomers were Alex, whom Francis had met, and Joey, and Brandon, the one who got the name everyone coveted. He and Joey were settled, but Brandon fled from Uncle Milton, while Joey was warned to leave before his neighbourhood was nuked.

After lunch, they wondered what it would be like with seven of them singing. So, they sang for a while. This time, it was Joey who compared it to the cat's purr.

They turned the telly back on, and Percy was holding the remote, surfing the channels.

'There's where the cat went,' he said.

There on the presenter's desk, the cat was purring into the microphone. The presenter was trying to give an analysis of the stock market.

He wasn't seeing the humour in it as did the newscasters a few days before. 'You really have to do something with that cat,' he said. 'Throw it down the rubbish shoot. Something! I hope the incinerator is on.'

A hand reached in from off camera and took the cat.'

The presenter looked like he was trying to recover his nerves. 'I *hate* cats!'

Then he started again. 'As I was saying, the bankers' forum has submitted their findings, saying that the present situation is the result of years of overindulging the weaker sectors, particularly - *DAMMIT!*'

'Meow.'

Then the presenter began saying things that, even in this day and age, aren't said on TV. Then he stormed off the set, while the cat purred long and loud into the mike for the entire nation to hear.

Then, it stopped, looked straight into the camera and said, 'Meow.'

It jumped off the desk.

The adverts came on.

'Meow.' Now it was standing in the door to the corridor. It turned towards the front door, looked at the boys and again said, 'Meow.'

Chapter 13

Joey opened the door for the cat, and the boys followed it out and down the street.

Around the corner was an abandoned construction site. There was a wire fence that was supposed to keep people out, but with a little pushing here and pulling there, there was a gap just right for Oscar's height and build. Then, a gap between a concrete beam and the wall should have taken them to the other side of the beam, but instead, there was an open area where a lot of people seemed to be camping out.

The cat stopped. The boys stopped. The people, men, women, children, old folks, sitting around, some in tents, but all with everything they owned, looked at the group of boys who all looked alike.

The cat turned around and meowed.

Francis started the first line:

Blessed are the poor, the blind, the lame, the trodden down...

The poor, the blind, the lame and trodden down stared as the boys made their way through the middle of their city park cum campsite.

At the far end of the park, along the main road, was a long row of police vans, and a large group of police poised to begin moving not-so-happy campers away.

Over to one side again were a group of journalists with cameras rolling - at least they had started rolling when they noticed the band of look-alike choir boys approaching. The campers were now also more interested in the boys than the row of police that were ready to pounce.

When they had finished all eight stanzas, the cat had led them around some bushes, and they came out in an alley, also crowded with settlers and squatters. It took all eight stanzas again to reach the other end of the alley. As they went, the campers looked more and more emotional. Some were weeping.

Francis felt like they were purring more strongly than ever. He also noticed there were a lot more than just the seven of them

At the far end there was a back door, through which the cat led them. Inside, however, the plate glass windows showed they were about 100 stories up. They appeared to have crashed a massive cocktail party.

Through eight stanzas again, the boys passed through a vast throng of people dressed to their teeth in tuxedos and gowns, holding their martinis and other drinks shaken-not-stirred. As they approached the other end of the vast room, people were either weeping or very upset.

A very rich important looking man behind a podium who thought that he was supposed to be giving a speech, looked especially miffed, and was calling for security.

There were security people, but none of them got very close.

The door at the end led into a TV studio, apparently one the cat had been to.

Somebody said, 'Look what the cat brought in!'

They managed to go slowly enough to make eight stanzas do for the length of the room, and by the end, nobody was being so light-hearted.

The door at the other end brought them to a bridge over a river that was no longer serving as a bridge, but a giant squatter community. They went the length of that bridge going through all eight stanzas several times.

At the opposite end they came to another tent city that wasn't actually adjoining the bridge. From there, onto a city street, where they saw a whole row of riot police with plastic shields poised on their right, and on their left, an angry looking mob of people in red bandanas. They looked less and less angry as they went, and some dropped the bricks and bottles they had been preparing to throw. Many also started weeping, including riot police.

Francis, for one, thought they were doing an awful lot of walking and singing. However he was surprised how energised he felt from their singing.

However, the cat apparently thought they needed a rest. At another cocktail party, this one a little bit more friendly, they were allowed to sit at a couple of big tables and were served as many tiny sandwiches and sausages on sticks, and cheese on crackers with caviar as they could eat.

Francis heard someone who looked like a journalist ask, 'Why do you all look alike?'

One kid, Francis couldn't tell who, said, 'We're all the same kid from different parallel universes.'

To a different question Francis didn't catch, someone answered, 'I don't know. You have to ask the cat.'

The cat was eating smoked salmon.

They went from there to more tent cities, more squatter communities and shanty towns, more riots and other similar situations, newsrooms, cocktail receptions, and other places where crowds of the type of people who needed it the most, heard them.

At some point, they entered a room full of empty beds, where they slept for a few hours. There was food waiting for them when they woke up, then, more tent cities, more riots, more newsrooms and other situations.

Now, they had come to a mostly empty park, and the cat stopped there. There were a lot of benches surrounding a fountain that, surprisingly, was turned on. The boys all sat on the benches.

Francis had met up with Percy again, the two having picked each other out by the clothes they were wearing, and they sat together.

'How many of us are there anyway?' he asked.

'Looks like about twenty.'

They were all dressed in clothes Francis recognised from his own wardrobe, in jeans, joggers, polo shirts, tee-shirt, button up shirts, their school uniform; all looked exhausted, but happy.

It looked like the cat was going up to one or another of them and leading them away. Sometimes two at a time.

One other boy was sitting on the other side of Percy.

'What's your name?' Percy asked him.

'I'm Oscar, like everyone else.'

'Didn't you choose a different name to tell you apart from the other Oscars?'

'No, never met any other ones till today, when we were singing.'

'Did you ever go down the stairs down in the cellar or on the top floor?'

'Been told not to go there,' said Oscar.

'Best if you don't,' said Percy. 'You'll get lost in a whole bunch of parallel universes, like we did.'

'How did you find us?' asked Francis.

'I was playing in the backyard, and the cat meowed at me, and ran into the bushes. I just went after the cat, got under the bush, but came out at the park full of people camping out, and there you all were. I just joined you singing, coz that's my favourite song from Mr. O'Brian's.'

Just then, the cat came up to the one talking, and meowed.

'I think it's gonna take you home now,' said Percy.

The boy got up and followed.

Francis asked Percy what he'd been longing to ask him. 'You knew about a lot of this all along, didn't you - like, that my home world was nuked and stuff?'

'Not that much. I sort of knew about your home world, but didn't know how to tell you without freak'n you out. Other than that, I just knew you and me were gonna do something special together. I think this was it.'

'But you knew your homeworld would get nuked, didn't you.'

'I just had a really bad feeling. Didn't know how to say it, so I got rid of you. I could have took you with me, but I think there's stuff you were supposed to do, and you did it.'

Another boy had been walking around the circle, saying or asking something. When he got to the boys in the bench nearest to them he heard what he was asking. 'Are you Francis?'

'No.'
'Are you Francis?'
'No, I'm Patrick.'
'Are you Francis?'
'No.'
He got to Francis.
'I'm Francis.'

'Hi. I'm the one you rescued from Uncle Milton. Megan told me your name is Francis and that I owe you big time. Anyway, thank you, and I'm sorry about Percy.'

'That's Percy. He got away before the nuke came down. The cat warned him.'

'Wow! Hi Percy.'

'Hi.'

'Your parents are really cool.'

'They weren't my original parents. I just found them.'

The cat walked up to him and meowed.

Francis said, 'There, the cat's gonna take you home again. Say hi to Megan for me.'

'I will,' he said as he went off after the cat.

Chapter 14

The cat approached Percy and Francis, standing equal distance between, and meowed. They both got up and followed.

They reached the end of the park, walked into a neighbourhood Francis thought he recognised, but wasn't near a park.

Francis turned and looked behind him. There was no park. Only the primary school, where it always was.

Just ahead, he recognised the newsagent where he always stopped to buy sweets on the way home from school (whenever he had any money). He'd been there just the other day with Uncle Benjamin and his cousins.

But this time there was something wrong. From about twenty metres beyond the newsagent, all the houses looked partly burnt, windows blown out, some in ruins, some not standing at all.

'This world got Nuked!' said Percy.

'Why is he bringing us here then?'

'Donno.'

Up ahead they could see their house. Of all the houses, it seemed to be in the best shape.

Both boys were gazing up at it so they didn't notice who was standing nearby.

'Dad, look! Oscar!'

'Er - which one?'

There was Dad, Mum and Megan standing outside the house. Some people that looked like engineers were going in and out of the house with clipboards and measuring tapes.

Both boys ran to them, both saying, 'Mummy! Daddy!'

'A miracle!' said Mum.

'Woah, there's two of you!' said Dad, 'when we thought we'd lost the one!'

'Were there not a couple dozen of them on the telly?' said Mum.

Francis said, 'I have to explain something to you. Those stairs in the cellar and the one up on the top floor, they go to parallel universes…'

It took a while, but they explained it, and Mum and Dad finally accepted the existence of parallel universes and very wise cats; the ultimate proof, of course, being the two Oscars (not to mention the dozen or so on the telly).

Because they and Francis remembered the exact same events leading up to the nuke and Francis' disappearance, it was confirmed that this was Francis' home world. Because Percy seemed to be hopelessly lost from his homeworld (apparently the cat thought so - speaking of which, where was the cat?) he would stay as his twin brother.

They had walked to Granddad's house and were sitting in his lounge.

'So, you're Percy,' said Dad.

'Yeah.'

'And you like the name "Percy"?'

Percy nodded.

'How about you take the middle name of Shelly. You can be named after another literary figure.'

'His wife, Mary Shelly, wrote *Frankenstein*, you know,' said Megan.

'We can call you Mary then!' haughed Francis.

'No way!' laughed Percy. 'I'll stick with Percy Shelly.'

'How 'bout Percy Bysshe Shelly?' said Megan. 'That's his whole name. That way you can have an extra middle name.'

He agreed.

And the other Oscar kept 'Francis' as a second middle name.

The electric was on at Granddad's house. According to the news, the group of identical looking boys had shown up singing in at least three places in the last two days. It was one of the top stories.

Opinions ranged from this being an angelic visitation to a very cleverly made up group of child actors. They certainly couldn't be siblings, as no womb could have given birth to so many at once. Clones? A possibility.

Someone had also pointed out that the cat leading them looked like the same as had visited a newscast, and appeared at the peace talks.

Because of the change in the general atmosphere, the angel theory was the popular one.

The old house was going to be repaired. The insurance company, which had been holding back for this reason or that, had just relented an hour before, and sent some people out to look at the house.

Both Francis and Percy thought it was the result of their singing.

The changes of the next few days seemed to confirm their opinion. The very rich seemed to have become more generous, people were getting their jobs back, people were being allowed back onto their property on extensions of deadlines and reductions of their loans; the nation was suddenly in a better mood. So were the 'noble neighbours'.

Soon, Oscar and Percy were back in school. They weren't sure what explanation their parents gave for there being two of them. A few of their old classmates were, sadly, missing.

Finally, they moved back into their old house. The boys' room had a double bed.

Oscar was awakened by the cat jumping onto the bed. It settled down between the two boys and purred. Oscar fell back to sleep.

He dreamed that the cat got up, walked to the foot of the bed and turned around and looked at them. It started to grow in size until it was as big as a lion, and an unusually large lion at that.

It was a lion.

Wings grew out of its back. In fact, three sets of wings - six wings in all. The lions head morphed to that of an eagle, and again into that of an ox, and then into that of a majestic looking man, and then back to a lion again as it repeated the cycle. When it became a man again, he spoke in a voice that seemed to echo against far away mountains, 'Blessed are the pure in heart, for they will see Him who is Most Holy.'

At that, the creature spread its wings and flew into a light that had become visible behind it. As it flew, the light became brighter than the sun, many times brighter than the nuke Oscar had seen in his imagination. He could see the creature join three other creatures of the same kind, who surrounded that light with the tips of one of their sets of wings touching. He could barely make out a figure in the midst of the light, with a face that smiled at him. It was a smile that seemed to do the same thing as a hug.

Oscar awoke, and it was dark. The cat had gone.

He heard Percy whisper, 'Wow!'

'Did you see that too?'

'Yeah!'

They didn't see the cat again for a long time.

Appendix

For You the World Was Made

by Boz O'Brian

Blessed are the poor, the blind,
the lame, the trodden down
With the poor and contrite spirit,
there I will be found
Yours is the Kingdom of Heaven,
do not be afraid
The earth is your inheritance,
for you the world was made

Blessed are those that mourn,
for I will comfort you
Those who come home weeping, praying
as I bring you through
I will lead by streams of water,
along smooth paths I've laid
The earth is your inheritance,
for you the world was made

Blessed are the meek, whose only
hope is in the Lord
When evildoers are cut off,
the wicked are no more
You will inherit the land,
in peace that will not fade
The earth is your inheritance,
for you the world was made

Blessed are you who hunger now
for things that ought to be
Thirst for justice, mercy served,
the oppressed all set free
You will see your dream come true,
your hunger will be stayed
The earth is your inheritance,
for you the world was made

Blessed are the merciful,
my mercy you will know
Mercy will win over judgement,
you'll reap what you sow.
Mercies new come every morning,
for you the table's layed
The earth is your inheritance,
for you the world was made

Blessed are the pure in heart,
my pureness you will see
To love the Lord with all your heart,
your mind, all you can be
He is One, and with one heart
you'll see, be not afraid
The earth is your inheritance,
for you the world was made

Blessed are those who make peace
My own child you shall be
A tongue that spreads discord I hate
My way is unity
The God of peace and harmony,

that is your DNA
The earth is your inheritance,
for you the world was made

Blessed are you when you get flack
for seeking what is right
They call you names, they lock you out
for following the light
The coming kingdom is your share so
do not be afraid
The earth is your inheritance,
for you the world was made

Note on navigating the parallel worlds from Oscar's house: The secret to getting back to the world you just came from is to remember that if you go in a circle of five, three moves in one direction, and two in another, you'll be passing the same five worlds. Percy simplified it for Francis by saying that to get back to the world you just came from, you make three moves back in that direction, and one in the other direction. However, it doesn't have to be in that order, as long as you leave the world you're in in the direction you came from, and on the forth move, you enter the destination world from the opposite direction from where you left it (meaning if you left by the cellar, you'll arrive by the attic, and vice versa. So, instead of going down three times (or up three times), you could go down twice, up twice, and down again; or down once, up three times and down.

Visit my website *www.RobbyCharters.co.uk* and download this one for free...

The Wrong Time

A collection of short stories, noveletts and some flash fiction

* A filmmaker of the future, using a new untested medium, gets tangled up in his story in ***The Filmmaker and the Sceptre;***

* The fantasy to end all fantasies: ***The Genie;***

* Time Dialation works in mysterious ways in ***The Last Shall be First;***

* a multi-universe ghost story in which Geoffrey literally finds himself in ***The Wrong Track*** - ;

Novellette: *The Wrong Time* - Sean O'Riley gets pulled through a vortex and finds himself married to his best friends wife. How does a proper, down to earth business man who only reads "mundain" fiction, go about finding his way back to his own time? He does, but he picks up some luggage along the way...

The flash fiction: From a physics class of the future: what is a "flong"? in ***The Flong Files***

More flash fiction, including an alternative history of Little Red Riding Hood, a sequel to The Pied Piper (a proper horror story), and an experiment in time travel and second person narration ...

Readers Comments at Amazon:

"...Kudos to the author for a readable, well-researched, original and inventive collection..."

" ...is a thoroughly intriguing and enjoyable collection of short stories by Robby Charters, tied together with a ribbon of twisted time..."

"...fantastic. Thoroughly entertaining, retains interest, and had a great grasp on scientific theory..."

Download it free when you visit my website: *www.RobbyCharters.co.uk*

fine print: you may receive an email or two (or three...) from yours truly with news about my books. But I'll try not to sound spammy -- promise!

Other books by Robby:

Pepe - In a world of flying magnetic trains & floating cafés he lives in a derelict construction site with his sister, cleaning windscreens at an intersection. He doesn't know who he really is. That fact could cost him his life - or it could be the key to the future of Cardovia, where futuristic technology blesses only the rich, but the poor are left scraping. Also available as a graphic nove.

Orphand of Space-Time - When he was nine, Drake Johnston was sure he had a best friend named Timmy. But Timmy never existed, and everyone thought he was Drake's imaginary friend. Many years later, when Drake looks further, he finds himself on the trail of a dangerous assassin. He has help from Johann, a member of an ancient Order of Timekeepers, whose mandate is to keep history on the right track, preventing mass destruction and genocide when they can.

Eetoo - At seems like humanity has very little to justify its existence, until one small facet falls into place. Then, it suddenly makes sense...

Eetoo, a primitive shepherd boy on an obscure planet embarks on a mission to seek the birthplace of humaity. He has help from other interplanetary humans and other intelligent creatures, as well as opposotion. Some still remember the atrocities committed by the human galactic empire in the past. Eetoo has fundamental questions about his own species.

The Zondon - They are extraterrestrial, but they've been born as ordinary humans with only a residue of their memory. Their mission to save the galaxy began before they were born to these bodies. They just have to find themselves and get to it. But the enemy is ready and waiting…

The Eurasian - Late 21st century America is ruled by multinational corporations hiding behind a veneer of virtual reality. Also behind that veneer is the great American outback - a patchwork of independent republics, some Nazi, some Native American, Mafia kingdoms, millitant Christian states, redneck cowboy states and more...

A group of Asian students on an international tour stumble into that outback. But can they get out again?

The Story of St. Catrick - Dr. Catrick, a professor at the Feline University in Catropolis had a life changing experience as a young cat that set him on his mission in life, to proclaim that animal species can and should live in harmony. All the while, the rodents are rising up against cat rule. Catrick and his friends encounter political agendas, prejudices, and countless other reasons for not doing the obvious.

Printed in Great Britain
by Amazon